Jesús

Peter Baker was born in Eas
began his writing career towa
World War. He created the innovative and influential film magazine of the sixties, *films and filming* and represented Britain on the juries of many international film festivals, including those at Berlin, Cannes, Moscow and Venice. He has contributed to several television series and his previous novels include *To Win a Prize on Sunday, Cruise, Casino, Clinic, Bedroom Sailors* and *Babel Beach.* He lives in Málaga, Spain.

Jesús

Peter Baker

Millivres Books
Brighton

First published in 1998 by Millivres Books (Publishers)
33 Bristol Gardens, Brighton BN2 5JR, East Sussex, England

A CIP catalogue record for this book is available from the British Library

ISBN 1 873741 34 0

Typeset by Hailsham Typesetting Services, 2 Marine Road, Eastbourne, East Sussex BN22 7AU

Printed and bound by Biddles Ltd., Walnut Tree House, Woodbridge Park, Guildford, Surrey GU1 1DA

Distributed in the United Kingdom and Western Europe by Turnaround Distribution Co-Op Ltd., Unit 3, Olympia Trading Estate, Coburg Road, Wood Green, London N22 6TZ

Distributed in the United States of America by LPC Group, 1436 West Randolph Street, Chicago, Illinois 60607, USA

Distributed in Australia by Stilone Pty Ltd, PO Box 155, Broadway, NSW 2007, Australia.

The publishers wish to thank the heirs to the
Federico Garcia Lorca estate and to
Mercedes Casanovas Agencia Literaria
in particular for permission to use lines from
Lorca's classic dirge on the death of a matador
friend in Peter Baker's JESUS.

for

PETER

the Paul of this story
who, thanks be to God, is
still making me happy after
forty-five wonderful years

together

and for all the J.C.s
who have brightened our lives.

He that loveth not knoweth not God
for God **IS** love.

(1 John 4:8)

In the beginning . . .

THE DAY FRANCO died, Jesús was born. I remember the day well. The fierce sun beat down on the faded and blistered paint-work of my front door, which opened unfashionably onto the Málaga waterfront. On the other side of the harbour, in the main drag, a dozen or more *policia* in their shabby grey and red uniforms were scrambling like urchins in a desperate attempt to gather subversive literature before it could be seen by the late afternoon shoppers, who at any moment would appear like a swarm of bees roused from siesta. For if anything was certain in the old Spain, it was that the *caudillo* was the King of Kings: whereas Jesús, I was to discover some years later, had a propensity for becoming a quean of something-or-other.

A well respected Madrid newspaper recently informed readers that one-in-five women have their first boy-child christened Jesús. A phone call to the local jail elicited the fact that they currently have ninety-nine Jesúses behind bars. My postman is Jesús. There is a Jesús who works as a croupier in the Marbella casino: and only last week *Diario Sur* reported the the loss of a Jesús at sea because, when his trawler went down, he went down with it, instead of walking on the water. I know of no other people so obsessed by the prestige of knowing and the power of being the Son of God, that they are prepared to risk the wrath to come. Indeed, it is Black Spain.

But at the time of the *caudillo's* death I was unaware of J.C. mewling and puking in his mother's arms. I was still living with Paul, my lover for twenty-five years, unaware that leukaemia was soon to take him from me. No one dies on the Costa del Sol, we merely fade away, melt into the sunbaked, barren land where the lush foothills of Andalusia join the Mediterranean sea, the cradle of civilization. The Phoenicians pillaged the earth; but the Romans gave the people roads. The Moors conquered them; but left them learning. And the Reyes Católico both freed and debauched them, so that today this thin coastal strip is urbanized, publicized, and sodomized for *extranjeros* loaded with booze, booty and beauteous boobs. Yet little more than a jogger's stride inland are verdant vines, ageless olives, foraging fighting bulls and white-walled villages that snooze beneath a somnolent sun.

The widowed Tia Tula, who helps her married sister run the *posada* in Pavo, has started the day by burning the *magdalenas*. She is cursed by a *duende*, which only yesterday had her washing off the line, and caused her to sit on a chair that wasn't there after she had partaken of her morning sippers of sweet anise. A *duende* is the ghost of a child who has died before it can be baptized: and there are many such children in Pavo, because Father Ignacius is such a wicked priest. Jesús, who was born in Pavo, might have been able to do something about it because his *gitano* family know all there is to know about *el amor brujo*, blood weddings and other such things: but J.C. was too busy being the city-boy, stuck into *salas de fiesta*, blood and sand, computers, compact discs and fast cars he called *guapo*. The old men sit in the shade of the oleanders in the Plaza de la Constitucion (formerly José Antonio, formerly just the *plaza*) and nod their heads. This they know to be true, because their forefathers told them so.

ECCE HOMO! *(St. John 19:5)*

THE TWO THICK ladies were struggling with their cross, as they had done every day for the past twenty-two years, ever since Rafael was born with a substandard telephone exchange that failed to send the right signals to his muscles.The ginger-haired lady had been widowed a few months after Rafael's birth; and her unmarried sister had joined her from the north, so that Rafael might grow up in a home, and not an institution. He was overweight from being confined to the wheel-chair; and every day the cross became heavier, more daunting, as it had to be negotiated down the treacherous flight of stairs from the old apartment opposite mine, to the street. Of course, there was always someone to help: but their independence was such that they always insisted on doing something just as burdensome in return, like repairing my torn sheets. And last night they'd sure got torn!

"I may see you later, Raf," I told him. "I'm watching the processions tonight. Maybe, I'll get religion!"

"We have seats in the Alameda," the mother beamed. She tried lifting her son's head from where it lolled on his shoulder but he'd been over-sedated, and the movement did little more than produce an outflowing of saliva from the parted lips.

The wet mouth indecently reminded me of the hunky young plate-layer's wet mouth of the night before. I felt a momentary flush of shame, not because of the physical pleasure the other had provided but because it hadn't satisfied, in the way wet mouths round nothing more depraving than the first of the season's cantaloups would have satisfied with Paul. I'd told Raf I might get religion. If I was honest, I'd have told him I might get another cock. That was the reason I milled around every night with the crowds celebrating Semana Santa. I knew what was happening to me. I was trying to work Paul out of my system. By the end of the week it would all be over, he'd be over, and I could start life again. I let the image of yesterday's RENFE hunk send the blood throbbing down my penis, saw the blood of a waxen Christ lunge at me from a cloud of incense, and recovered my poise with a private joke. It had never occurred to me before that the Compagnie International des Wagons Lits had catered for the Last Supper.

"Well, now, there's a remedy for everything except death," Paul would say, quoting the Knight of the Sad Countenance every time things got screwed up; and together, we'd set about unscrewing them.

Paul had drifted into oblivion three years ago. We had been inseparable. Our love had grown from the dunghill of lust and had perpetually blossomed because neither legal sanctions in our teens, nor the delights of gay-adultery in our maturity, had deflected us from a shared belief that total confidence in the loved one in all things, conquered all. One flesh, divided by death, I hadn't found it easy to adjust; but I knew it wouldn't be Paul's wish that I should cut myself off from the living world and get me to a monastery. So that as I lay on my bed last night, sixty-nining the muscular young railway man, I wasn't surprised to sense Paul enjoying it with me. We so often talked to each other when apart in life, it seemed illogical not to do so when apart in death. But what had surprised me were the eyes. As I looked over the landscape of the sex-partner's solid thighs, in the dim light at the far end of the of the room I was certain I saw a pair of eyes watching, wanting, but unable to make contact. "Paul, is that you?" I'd breathed: but my vision was obscured by pubic hair, and when I came up for air, the eyes had gone.

I heard the muffled beat of the drums and the acrid incense were tingling my nostrils before I'd got halfway across the park. Six *cofradias* were processing tonight, each starting from its holy shrine and returning to the shrine some five, or six, hours later, having taken in the four corners of the ancient city. The vast *tronos*, each weighing several tons and bearing either an effigy of the crucified Jesús, or the mother, Mary, were encrusted with gold-leaf, gilt or yellow paint, according to the affluence of its sponsors. They were carried from within by a hundred, or more, men and boys, each remunerated for his services, preferably in cash, less preferably in Mother Church's indulgence – rough porters from the central market, students in their blue serge suits, devout bank clerks, devious office boys. The *nazarenos*, anyone who thought himself, or herself, important in this world, had paid for the privilege of processing with their particular *cofradia*, anonymous in hooded robes, theatrically spectacular in both colour and design, the whole scene lit by ten thousand flickering candles.

"You want nice souvenir, *señor*?"

I'd had my eyes on the nape of the young man's neck for much too long, unable to take them off as I was pleasantly aroused by his thick pelt of glistering black hair, which duck-arsed over smooth olive skin, framed by a violent green shirt only youth would dare to wear. When the boy turned to face me, compelled to do so by some gut instinct that told him he was being observed, I saw he was carrying a tray stacked with wooden crosses and crucifixes. I was to learn later that his father made them: and that he made wooden donkeys for Christmas, wooden flowers for All Souls, and, in between, turned out everything from briar pipes to hardwood dildos for sale along the Costa.

"Yo no es un turista," I told him.

"You rich. Much money," he said. "Me poor. No money."

I was on the verge of asking in his own language if he had a *gordo pollo* that needed attention; but something told me he was not rent. There was an aura about the young man I find difficult to describe: it was as though he was protected by some person, or some thing.

Instead, I said, "Where did you learn to speak English? In bed?"

I don't think he understood, he certainly didn't get the bed bit, but when he realized I was trying him out, his serious, oval face broke into, I thought, too eager a smile. "You give me lessons, please, *señor*," he said. "Very important I speak English. I have books. I pay."

Had I known the outcome then, I wouldn't have been so

rash as to reach over the heads of a group of women guzzling *churros* at a sidewalk café and pull a paper serviette from the dispenser. As I scribbled my address, I told myself my intentions were of the most honourable. I needed to earn some money. Fast. It was, after all, no more than a *quid pro quo*. Paul knew his long illness had stymied our contacts with the spaghetti-western producers further along the coast at Almeria, where Paul would sit in the sun (behind the camera) and I would sit in the shade (hopefully, improving the words the actors had to say on a battered bird-cage of a typewriter).

"Come next week. *Proximo semana*," I told him, giving him his first lesson. "*A las cinco de la tarde!* Five! Bull fight time!"

He was still blabbering his gratitude, as high up on a balcony overlooking the Plaza de la Merced, a *flamenco* singer was penetrating the night air with his *saeta* for the Virgin. Nearer the cathedral, I saw a procession led by over-barbered Guardia Civil officers, their drawn swords painted a matt black. Every few minutes, a high pitched bell would signal a rest break and there would be a rush for the nearest bar, the penitents to down a little *copa* of brandy, the bearers to refill their *botas*, the leather wine skins they kept on hooks in the secret underbelly of the *trono*. Hucksters were selling their popcorn, dips were picking pockets, and old ladies were shedding tears.

"If he was alive today, no one would bother to crucify him," Paul had said a few years before his death, when we had stood in this very place watching the Easter processions, together. "The tabloids would pick up the suffer the little children bit and he'd be accused of child abuse, or something worse. Like being gay."

Paul was very close to me tonight. I saw his eyes watching me from the deep recesses of every penitential hood. Outside the law courts, a mob was shouting its praise of a petty villain released to join the procession, a present-day Barabbas. Black velvet robes. The gut-turning roll of a hundred drums. Bare flesh of the macho legionnaires. An unemployed youth shouts insults at the figure of the crucified, throws a stone, chips a waxen cheek. Ungentle police drag protester from lamp-post and deliver eye-for-eye and tooth-for-tooth with loaded truncheons. A *nazareno* raises his hood to vomit from too much fear, or booze. Under his robe, a silk suit and hand-made shoes, faint shadow of those penitents of yore with their bare feet and blooded backs. Hooded, so not to display their dark love, they had flagellated themselves to fulfilment, just as today some gay brothers can only express their love through pain.

I was wondering if there would be a market for a crown of thorns among the SM toys on display in the international sex-shops, when something that looked for all the world like a giant duck in a purple robe, waddled towards me. Two plump hands reached up and wrestled with the hood. I saw the brightly painted, badly split fingernails and realized it was a woman who was about to present herself to me. I grasped the hood by its point, and pulled; but, to judge by the muffled screams, I was pulling hair as well as hood. Eventually, Mari-Carmen appeared, breathless, flushed and demanding.

"I was hoping to see you," she said. "I'm processing tonight and I've also got to do a piece on Douggie Hardman. Do you think you could cope with an interview?"

I'd known Mari-Carmen for little more than a month. She was the producer in charge of the English language programmes on Radio Independiente Plus. Unfortunately, she had what was possibly the most atrocious accent on the Costa, but as I was trying to curry favour with her in the hope that my previous microphone experience with the 'Beeb' would land me a job and some useful dough-ray-me, I wore the chivalrous cloak of the Knight of the Sad Countenance. 'She isn't a bad bit of goods, the Queen. I wish all the fleas in my bed were as good.'

"You know how to use one of these?" She was struggling to remove from under her robe a bulky piece of recording equipment the 'Beeb' had declared obsolete a couple of decades ago. "If you hold up a little placard, Douggie'll probably recognize you."

Most of the participants in the procession were watching me try to disentangle Mari-Carmen from the recording gear. I had a suspicion I was being sent-up by one of the Foreign Legion band boys. I was damned if I was going to hold up a placard, big or little, however much of the local plonk Hardman shipped back to the UK.

"Can't I hold up the little drummer boy?"

"Oh, you *are* awful!" she said, quickly hiding her embarrassment under her hood.

I found Rafael and the two thick ladies eating ice cream. "Are you enjoying the processions?" I asked.

Only after I'd asked did I realize what a damned silly question it was. How could anyone *enjoy* an execution? Rafael's eyes were sparkling in a way I had never seen before, as his sub-standard telephone exchange struggled to tell me how he had been wheeled the length of the Alameda by the Real Hermandad de Nuestra Senora de la Piedad.

"We're thinking of taking him to Lourdes later this year," the mother said.

Suddenly, I was aware that Rafael had reached out and was holding my hand. It went through me like an electric shock and I blew a fuse. "I've just been given a job to do," I said. "We'll talk about Lourdes some other time."

Could it be the eyes of yet another plaster Jesús that penetrated the back of my head as I tried to lose myself in the milling crowd? I couldn't get away from eyes tonight, real, or imaginary, or glass. I was being forced to ask myself questions to which I had no answers. I hated these public celebrations of Easter for just that reason. Why did a man named Jesús have no brothers, or sisters? Was his carpenter dad gay? Was Jesús gay? He was executed, aged thirty-two, without having wife or child. Surely it was a miracle the world survived at all, with men and women on it to form a church, any church, if that was the example of procreation they were expected to follow. Did a Rafael hold his hand, as the boy had just held mine? Or did he hold his cock? Did Jesús and his fishers-of-men express themselves with no physical contact whatsoever? Did not their love for each other grow, as my dead lover's love for me had grown and mine for him, from our awareness that we were made in the image of God, that our bodies, with which we expressed our universal love of life, were truly the temporary habitats of our souls? Or had God made only a plaster effigy of man, to be chipped by a yobbo's thrown stone, so that for eternity man is left to make a god in his own image? *Ecce homo!* Or worship the sun, the phallus, or the golden calf? The solemn brass of the Foreign Legion band pounded my ears, my nostrils were ablaze with burning incense, my eyes filled with tears of doubt, as I allowed the multitude to carry me towards the Puerta Nuevo. Why was Jesús a 'he' and not a 'she'? Was he a hermaphrodite, a true bisexual? Why had no great artist painted a full frontal nude? What are the sins of the flesh if they are not the Crusades, the Papal Wars, the Somme, Hiroshima, and today's bloodshed almost any place on earth in the name of . . . God?

"Seco montes grande, por favor."

I had swung into the tiny bodega near the confluence of narrow roads at the Puerta Nuevo, desperate for a drink. Outside, two *tronos* had arrived simultaneously, vying for position to be first to head towards the snob stands in the Plaza de la Constitucion. The black-and-purple *nazarenos* were elbowing the white-and-gold *nazarenos*, while a couple of embarrassed municipal cops lurked in the background, hoping it wasn't going to end in a punch-up. A candle inadvertently set light to a penitent's robe. An onlooker obligingly extinguished the flame with a can of beer. It was impossible to get out of the bodega for the crush of multi-coloured *nazarenos* trying to get in. Fortunately, plonk king Douggie Hardman was crushing in with them. They stacked their hoods on the bar like sailors stack their hats and bald-headed Douggie, voice even louder than a Spaniard (which was no mean achievement) began ordering Scotch. It wasn't available. It never is available in this kind of establishment: and Douggie should have known it. I took an instant dislike to the man and had no doubt he would take an instant dislike to me.

"Mr. Hardman, will you say a few words for the Radio Independiente English programme, please?" I nearly upset his glass of the rough local brandy which had to substitute for the Scotch, thanks to the damned antiquated recorder.

"There's no such thing as a bad Spanish wine," Douggie said, launching into his sales spiel. "It's just that some wines are better than others,"

I recalled one of Paul's favourite maxims. If you can't comfort the afflicted, then at least you can afflict the comfortable. So I shoved the mike in Douggie's face and asked, "What does Jesús mean to you? Sir?"

I knew from the hostility in his eyes that tomorrow he would complain about me to Mari-Carmen. My chance of regular employment was disappearing like spit off a hot stove: but I stood my ground.

Douggie smiled uncomfortably and gulped his brandy. "He kept the wedding party going by turning water into wine, didn't he?" he said.

"You really believe that, sir? You believe in miracles?"

Fortunately for Douggie, he was saved by the bell. As soon as they heard the tinkling, the brotherhood of vintners grabbed their hoods and disappeared into the comforting anonymity of wealth. I suddenly felt alone in the crowd, in desperate need for someone to hold my hand. All my life I'd been asking the questions, the professional cynic. Was there nothing in which I believed? Yes, the sun would rise tomorrow. But could I be sure to wake to see it? And if I didn't wake . . . what? I stepped smartly aside to avoid walking on a printed cross on a Semana Santa poster that was blowing about on the pavement, and knocked into a dark-eyed young man as I did so. He smiled, that knowing smile of recognition. He would hold my hand. But for once my cock did not give a beat of anticipation. He asked me the time and I pointed callously to the cathedral clock, leaving him to find another's hand to hold. How many times throughout the world tonight was the cry of rejected love going up to the stars? *'My God, my God, why hast thou forsaken me?'*

I returned to my apartment just in time to see the two

thick ladies struggling with their cross. Rafael was holding a packet in his lap. I took the weight of the wheel-chair at his feet, while the two women guided it backwards up the twisting staircase, one step at a time.

"Have you been buying *churros* for breakfast?" I asked. "They'll make you fatter than you are already!"

He could usually take a ribbing from me. Like all invalids, he'd come to terms with his disability; or so I thought. But tonight there were tears in his eyes. It was a night for tears; in the far distance, we could still hear the beat of muffled drums. I could recall too many occasions in the past when I had given Paul cause for tears. His eyes had been like Rafael's eyes. Soft. Brown. Deep pools of desire.

"I'm afraid Rafael has been molesting you," the mother said, dragging the wheel-chair up another step.

Molestar. It was an odd choice of word. To annoy, molest. To trouble. So often, I'd been afraid of troubling them. Hunky sex-partners tearing the sheets, for a start.

"We've bought Rafael a lock and chain for his chair," she went on. "I'm afraid he's started walking in his sleep. He could distress us all . . . if anything happened."

Tears were streaming down Rafael's cheeks now. The apartment door I'd left off the latch for the dishy bit of last supper. The eyes watching us in the dark had been Rafael's eyes! Yearning. Longing for something beyond his reach. Crying out from the confines of his imprisoned body, 'Am I, too, not made in his image?' And the hollow answer, floating back on the muffled drums across the city: God—is—L-O-V-E . . . God—is—L-O-V-E . . . love . . . love . . . lo . . . l . . .

JUDGE NOT . . . *(St. Matthew 7:1)*

TO QUOTE THE Knight of the Sad Countenance, as Paul would have done, 'Hunger is the best sauce in the world.' The days following Easter were so busy wheeling and dealing in order to regain lost ground, foodwise, that I completely forgot about the young *gitano* who was going to contribute a few pesetas in return for English lessons.

"Tio Mac liked your piece on Douggie Hardman, so I think you're in if you can come up with a programme format that doesn't cost the earth," Mari-Carmen told me.

Tio Mac is how Señor Don Alvarez José Macasoli, the station manager of Radio Independiente Plus, is affectionately, or contemptuously, known to the staff. I sensed Mari-Carmen, who used to be his secretary, fell into the affectionate lobby, so I decided to fall in with her.

"How soon do you think I can start?"

"We're building up our English language hatch, match and dispatch tape library," she told me. "It doesn't pay much, but it gives you an entrée to everybody whose anybody on the Costa."

"That's fine by me." I held her handbag while she lit a cigarette. She immediately began coughing.

"You don't, do you?" she said. I had a feeling she was desperate for some other fellow creature to share her addiction. "Maybe I wouldn't if they stopped them coming in from the Rock."

Gibraltar, scarcely a rock's throw from the Costa, has long been a thorn in the Spanish side, ambivalent about its part in the constant flow of drugs and contraband from North Africa to southern Europe and beyond, and seemingly indifferent to the human misery that lack of control creates. The minnows of misery flog their packs of duty-free fags to drivers of vehicles large and small, public or private, paused perilously (for the minnows) by the lights at busy traffic junctions; while bigger fish deal in deeper waters, from Estepona in the west to Nerja in the east, purveying their pleasure poisons – crack, coke, ecstasy, what glamour! – to the living dead.

"I'd smoke, if they did anything for me," I told her truthfully. "I tried them when I was a cub reporter on a provincial newspaper in the UK; but I was always leaving them about unfinished, till eventually I set fire to the news editor's office and faced the stark choice. Job. Or habit."

We were having our morning coffee in a cafeteria frequented by Málaga's media people in the Alameda de Colon. It was getting unpleasantly crowded inside, while outside the palm trees were rustling in the early morning breeze and sending shafts of sunlight dancing on the baroque buildings opposite. Like many old buildings in the city centre, two of them were empty shells, the facades compulsorily preserved while their interiors were rebuilt to modern standards. But before that could happen, much to the chagrin of many an *empresa* there might be a delay of weeks, months, years even, for an archeological dig into Málaga's Roman past. When they get round to rebuilding my old apartment they expect to find the Roman fish market.

"This is on me," Mari-Carmen was saying. "You can buy me a real meal when your cheques start coming through. In the meantime, I'll fix for you to do a piece on old Luis Molier."

"The legal eagle?"

She smiled, and in her atrocious accent, added, "But don't tell him it's for an obituary . . . or he'll lay an egg!"

I returned to the apartment to find a call waiting for me on the answering machine. The mechanised voice announced itself as that of an almost forgotten school chum, one Max Hassler, now apparently a partner in the swish fine arts dealers, Northleigh of Mayfair. I had been traced via a mutual school chum, still in harness for the 'Beeb'. Would I show him the Costa in ten days' time and please to fax my recommended list of Málaga galleries now. Or sooner. I was trying to remember Max, and all I could dredge up was a pale, undernourished boy still in short trousers conducting some obscene experiment behind the bike shed that involved an assortment of elastic bands and the school cat (which had been neutered anyhow), when Rafael's mum burst in. She was in such a state of breathless indignation that it was a good five minutes before I could understand a word she was trying to say. Eventually, she blurted out that the Policia Municipal had taken the Harley as it was parked where a *caseta* was wanted for a road safety exhibition. I looked out. Sure enough, there was a stick-on red triangle on a *paseo* kerbstone to prove the *grua* had done its worst. Damn, damn, damn, it would take the rest of the day and umpteen thousand pesetas I could ill afford to recover my pride-and-joy.

My interview with Don Luis Molier was quite different to what I'd expected of a Spanish legal eagle. For one thing, he was French by birth; for another, he had what most people would regard as a lop-sided view of crime.

"To turn an interesting thief into a tedious honest man is not necessarily a good idea," Don Luis said. "The world still fails to understand that sin is of itself a suffering. A crime can be a beautiful, almost holy thing. It could be argued that Our Lord loved the sinner as the nearest possible approach to perfection in man."

From morality, the subject drifted to art. "There are painters who can transform the sun into a yellow spot," Don Luis was saying. "But one must always be on the look-out for the painter who can turn a yellow spot into the sun."

"What's your opinion of Picasso, sir?" I asked. Pablo Picasso is Málaga's favourite son. His birthplace, in the north-east corner of the Plaza de la Merced, has thousands of tourists visiting it every week, oblivious of the fact that Pablo spent very few years of his life in Spain and left, vowing never to return while the Generalissimo was still alive. The dictator outlived the artist.

"It so happens that I have a Picasso. My wife's brother gave the family some financial assistance in the artist's youth." The old advocate was all circles of soft colour, as he sat in a leather-covered armchair, sucking a pipe and talking about angular modern art of clashing primaries. "My wife doesn't know I'm parting with it. It's a young male nude. It can be authenticated."

I was saying that the only original anything I'd owned was sin, when I heard Don Luis asking me to make some tentative inquiries on his behalf.

"But why me?"

"Because I trust you. I don't want the whole of the Costa del Sol to become cognisant of my affairs." Perhaps thinking I would refuse, he added, "There's ten per cent in it for you if the sale goes through."

Put like that, how could I refuse? But I wish I had. I was already committed to the embarrassment of meeting an old school chum of more decades ago than I cared to remember. When I found Max had checked into the four-star conformity of the Palacio Hotel I began to realize I was about to be used, that the only thing we now had in common was a few years shared experience, a long, long time ago. Paul had warned me on so many occasions when he was alive that there's no going back, and I knew he was right; but here I was, doing the very thing he'd warned me against. The evening Max arrived he was at a loose end so I agreed to show him the town. We finally got round to Manolo's Slipped Disc, where a decorate-a-friend's-buns contest was reaching its climax. Some twenty couples were busily engaged with water-soluble paints, artistically covering exposed flesh. Max seemed genuinely shocked. He stood in the centre of the disco, a suave, slightly greying man in a pale blue seersucker suit and hand-tied bow, almost spitting out his refusal of Manolo's invitation to be one of the judges.

"But it's not art!" he protested. "How can anyone be expected to make a valid judgement of such vulgarity?"

"You only had to say, and we could have left before the show started," I told him. "As far as I'm concerned, I prefer to feel fifty years young than fifty years old."

In the days that followed I had good reason to neglect Max. Selling a Picasso wasn't as easy as I thought it was going to be. I first went to John Truscott, the English dilettante who runs the fashionable Truscott Gallery in the Lanes. John is infamous for the women in his life, but in spite of knowing our disinterest in the female sex, he went out of his way to help Paul and myself when we first hit Málaga – almost literally so, by losing our way on our two-wheel transport and coming to an abrupt halt among the garbage bins in the cul-de-sac behind his gallery. John explained why he wasn't in the market for Picassos and suggested I had a word with Carlos Soler. John was not to know that the cautious Soler would have a word with a lot of other people, including the police. I was unceremoniously woken from siesta by two plain clothes Guardia Civil officers doubting the authenticity of the Picasso, doubting it was mine to sell, and warning of prosecution to come.

"We suggest, *señor*, that you consult a lawyer," the senior of the two men told me.

I did. I went straight to old Don Luis, on whose behalf I was trying to sell the damned thing. "You've got to get me off the hook," I demanded. "I don't expect a criminal lawyer to be a criminal."

"I daren't admit it's mine. My wife would make my life hell if she knew I was even thinking of parting with it." His poached-egg eyes filled with tears. "Her nagging would kill me."

"Old lawyers never die," I said. "They merely lose their appeal!"

I could never regard Mari-Carmen as a mother confessor, but I knew I had to warn my employers that the anchor-man of their new programme was about to be thrown to the wolves by a pillar of Spanish society who was scared of his wife's tongue and ashamed to admit he was trying to flog a very suspicious Picasso blue boy.

My producer thought it was awfully amusing. "Do show me! Do show me!" she cajoled. "Is it really a blue picture?"

"It was the artist's blue period." I told her, not that I have any claim to being an art critic. "He was hard up at the time and blue paint was cheap."

I thought I had offended her, but she threw me a lifeline. "I'll get Pippa to write a letter from the advertising department, saying they did it."

"What good will that do, except drop Tio Mac in it?"

"You were hawking it round the dealers, knowing it was a forgery, to test their integrity." The crow's feet round her eyes crackled with delight. "It will make a good item for the new programme."

I hung around the office while she got Pippa on the house phone. My Spanish is far from good, but it is good enough for me to pick up an undercurrent of intimacy between the two women. When Pippa joined us a few minutes later with a draft of the letter, I immediately felt the vibes generated between them. Pippa is a Basque: tall and slender, insinuating rather than walking into a room, her hair lush and shiny as is common in the rainy north, her tailored costume offset by a minimum of good jewellery. Younger than Mari-Carmen, she was everything my producer was not.

"Pippa would be in your shoes, if I hadn't persuaded Tio Mac to put her in charge of earning our daily bread," Mari-Carmen said.

I began to realize that Mari-Carmen was able to twist Tio Mac round her little finger and in all probability was the real power behind Radio Independiente Plus. "If the Guardia Civil swallow that, they'll swallow anything," I told Pippa after she'd read us the draft.

"They're not as fearsome as you think," Mari-Carmen said. "They like to have friends in the media, you'll see."

I thanked Pippa for her contribution to my well-being and returned to my apartment for some desperately needed shut-eye. I had no idea when I was likely to see Pippa again and, frankly, didn't care whether or not I ever saw her again; so, barely six hours later, I was somewhat thrown when she turned up at the Truscott Gallery for the champagne opening of an exhibition of paintings by contemporary Málaga artists. Max was also there, which was another surprise as I thought every minute of his time on the Costa would be taken up midst the flesh-pots of Marbella, evaluating items for Northleigh to auction.

"I hear you've upset the boys in green," Truscott said, handing me a catalogue.

"Storm in a tea-cup," I said, exchanging the catalogue

with a waiter for a glass of champagne.

"No investigation?" Truscott's eyebrows were raised. "That's unlike the Guardia. They're usually very thorough."

"If you don't believe me, you'll see it when the eggs are fried." Not for the first time had Cervantes' Knight come to my rescue.

There was a tense atmosphere which was at odds with the venue. I began to notice faces I had not seen on the gallery circuit before: and faces that were missing. Then, turning a corner by a rather bad *Atarazanas at Sunset,* I nearly had Pippa off her feet.

"We meet again," I said.

"I'm only here for the beer." She seemed amused by her command of English. But there was no disguising her discomfort at finding me there.

I found out why some half hour later when I went in search of Truscott to make my polite farewell. I found him in his inner sanctum. Pippa was there, too. They were in each others arms. I don't know who was the most embarrassed. I hate sharing guilty secrets, and to make matters worse, Max was still lurking.

"Doing a little business, old man," he said. He was looking decidedly guilty about the gills.

"*Here?* I thought you came to wheel and deal in Marbella."

"Found a pair of diamond ear-rings our mutual friend wants to give his latest lady love," Max said. "A brand new Ruskie capitalist with a cash flow problem. I was merely helping a fellow traveller learn the basics of western exchange rates."

"You ripped him off! God, you're a bastard!"

"You shouldn't say things like that, old man. No, you definitely shouldn't."

As I walked back through the lanes in the gathering twilight, I asked myself why I hadn't learnt the art of making money behind the bike shed, instead of worrying about what other kids did to the school cat. I was still trying to work out why Max had apparently made more of a success of life than I had, when I opened the apartment door to find the whole place looking as though a typhoon had struck. I quite expected to find the video, TV and word processor gone, but no, they were all there. Even a five thousand pesetas bank-note I keep hidden for emergencies inside the sleeve of a Cadinot porno (sorry, French art) video had not been taken – it had been discovered, and carefully placed on my bedside table under the water glass, where it could plainly be seen. What did it all mean? I went across to see Rafael's aunt and mum. They expressed surprise. No, they'd seen no strangers hanging about. No, they'd heard nothing as the typhoon struck. I think Raf was about to tell me something, but a quick shake of the mother's head froze him to silence. Like all Spaniards, they didn't want to get involved. In anything. There would be no probing into the unknown, even to help a friend. Such is the scourge of civil war that it scars generation after generation, the more marked when a dictator such as Francisco Franco imposes a life style of see-hear-and-speak only what I tell you to see-hear-and-speak with such ruthless determination. I satisfied hunger with a glass of *seco montes*, a hunk of bread and fresh goat's milk cheese, and fell asleep in the chaos, determined to sort out the why and wherefore in the morning.

Come the dawn and Mari-Carmen was on the line. "Are you doing anything tonight, Pedro?"

"House work." What, I wondered, was the sudden familiarity of the Pedro bit in aid of.

"Tio Mac thinks we need a man to complete the coverage of tonight's International Jewellery Trades conference ball."

"My place is like a typhoon has struck. Is it anything to do with your Guardia Civil friends?"

"Pippa and me – or should it be I? – have top table invitations. I wanted to do something nice for her. Tomorrow is her birthday."

Paul often accused me of being slow on the uptake, but there could be no doubt the way Mari-Carmen was talking. She and Pippa were lovers. Or rather, she loved Pippa, but did Pippa love her?

I tried once more to get some sense out of her about my

wrecked home. "Who can I contact in the Guardia to find out if they *did* do it?"

"Did do what, Pedro?"

"Wrecked my home!"

"Don't be so silly, the Guardia don't do things like that."

It was obvious I wasn't going to get any sense out of her, burglary-wise, so I told her yes (you silly old dyke) I need the money so I'll be there (and I only hope for your sake darling Pippa remains the apple of your eye).

"You do have suitable evening wear?"

"I'll come in drag, if necessary!" With that, I hung up on her.

I spent the morning getting straight and by lunch time was too exhausted to fix my own meal, so I splashed out on my favourite 'peasant restaurant' behind the central market, where they really know how to fry *calamares.* As I left the apartment, I had a strange feeling I was being followed. But by who? And why? Then, as I ate my meal, I became increasingly convinced a man eating at a corner table by himself was a policeman, that he was only pretending to eat, that he was keeping me under surveillance, that he was going to arrest me at any moment. Tourists don't realize that when they are having a good time on the beach at Torremolinos, shopping for souvenirs in Fuengirola, or dancing the night away in Marbella, they are protected from the unwanted attention of pimps, touts, and muggers by more men and women out of uniform than are seen wearing it. The twenty-four hour protection plan with which the security authorities cover the walk up to Gibralfaro would impress any military tactician. Taking into account the millions of tourists who visit Spain every year, very few are involved in . . . .The man eating at the corner table by himself had got up and left. Without paying his bill. The waiter was streaking after him, riding an upturned crate of oranges like a skate-board. *Olé!* Plain clothed policeman he most certainly was not. I told myself I was becoming paranoid.

I was about to ask for the cheque, when a heavily built man with a bushy black moustache and an outdoor complexion that seemed utterly drained of blood, leaving the skin tinted an olive green, sank onto the chair opposite me. "Have you seen one of these before?" he asked, opening his leather-bound Policia Nacional warrant card and thrusting it in my face.

"Yes," I said. I felt a sudden wave of panic pour over me at the sight of the word 'Inspector', but why, I had done nothing wrong.

"I want to ask you a few questions," the man said, careful not to let his voice carry to the next table. "You can either answer them here, or at the *comisaria extranjeros*."

I told him I'd do whatever I could to help, my mind simultaneously trying to sort out the jumble of the spurious Picasso and my wrecked apartment, to say nothing of the monumental bill to recover my pride-and-joy from the municipal police pound. I watched with growing fascination as the man reached into his right button-down shirt pocket and pulled out a carefully folded piece of paper which he proceeded to unfold.

"Is this your address?"

I heard myself saying 'yes' while a flood of recognition swept through my mind.

"And it is your handwriting?"

"Yes." It was the serviette on which I had scribbled my address for that damned *gitano* kid.

"Can you tell me how it came to be in the possession of one Jesús Cepillo Heredias?"

"Because I gave it to him!" I was beginning to get angry; if this copper was anything like his British equal he would start making snide remarks about whether, or not, I made a habit of giving my address to street boys. "There's no law against my inviting to my home anyone I choose, is there?"

"No, sir." The man could not be more polite. "But I must warn you that this person is at present in custody and is likely to be charged with a serious offense involving dangerous drugs."

Suddenly, it all clicked into place. "My apartment was broken into yesterday while I was out. I suppose that was your doing."

"I wouldn't know about that, sir," the inspector said. "If you wish to make a complaint you can do so at the *comisaria*."

It was slowly dawning that the police had nothing on me and wanted to give me the message, unofficially, that it would be best not to stir things up. Why send an inspector to interview me over lunch, instead of having me brought formally by a patrol car to the *comisaria*? "My place looks like a typhoon has hit it," I said.

He ignored the remark but reached out to recover the serviette on which was scrawled my address. "Evidence, sir," he said. "You will be available to give evidence to the court, I take it?"

"No you can't take it!" I felt my hackles rise. "The boy apparently needs help, not evidence flung at him."

The inspector's voice hardened. "In that case, sir, I shall have to consult my superiors, and you may be hearing from us again."

"And I shall have to consult my lawyer, and you most certainly will be hearing from me!" I had convinced myself I was in the right, it was damnable the trouble, worry and expense they had caused me. Police were the same the world over: big feet and little brains.

The IJT conference ball attracted the smart set, the criminal fraternity and a sprinkling of high-flying dealers in ice: if the ball wasn't for ever, the Costa mongers were set on making it seem that way. The five-star Don Aranda, set on a promontory between moon-lit palms with an unbroken view out to sea, was staging the event for the fifth year. Mari-Carmen was waiting for me in reception. She was at her most gushing.

"Pedro, my dear, we do appreciate you freeing us from the chores like this," she said. I wasn't at all charmed by being her dear and the request for my presence hadn't included a condition that I did all the work. I was about to make both points clear before she made a habit of taking me for granted, when Pippa joined us from the powder room. The first thing I noticed was the diamond ear-rings. Max had certainly made sure that lover-boy Truscott got a lot for his money.

"We must buy you a drink before we go in, Pedro," Mari-Carmen was saying.

Had it been anyone other than my employer, I would have told them what they could do with their ritzy drink; but I let the intrepid dyke lead on. All around were the long and the short and the tall of the international jewellery trade, freeloading on champagne and caviar and anything that was going that they could not afford to eat at home (not that all of them had homes).

"Isn't she a lucky girl?" my producer beamed, touching one of Pippa's ear-rings. "They were given her by an advertising rep for a Barcelona fashion house who are booking air time. But, of course, they're only paste."

Pippa was doing everything she could to avoid eye contact. I guessed she was praying like mad that I didn't say anything compromising. "Let's hope her luck doesn't run out," I said.

I would have said much more had Mari-Carmen not been with us and I sensed Pippa knew this. Her hands were so tightly clasped the knuckles were white. Fortunately for Pippa, the young waiter who served the drinks stood between us and she no longer had to avoid my eyes. Instead, I found myself looking at the nape of the young man's neck and was seeing again the *gitano* boy, the thick pelt of glistering black hair which duck-arsed over smooth olive skin. What did the inspector say his name was? Jesús. Christ, I was day-dreaming of giving the Son of God a tumble between the sheets! And why not? According to the story, he was born and lived like a man. A white man? A black man? Chinaman? Rich man, poor man, beggar man . . .

"I was saying, Pedro, why don't you ask the IJT press people to point out delegates who can speak English. It will save you time editing your tapes," Mari-Carmen said, breaking into my reverie.

"My tapes. Your editing." I wasn't going to let the damned woman load everything on me.

"You help me a little," she wheedled. "Please."

I gulped my drink and got away from them before I promised her the earth. A bouncy man with round glasses and a round smile, with a 'Press' label on his lapel, put me in touch with an Amsterdam diamond wholesaler.

"The trouble with simulated crystals is that they are quickly tarnished by sulphur vapours in the town air," he was saying, but the whole time he spoke my mind was on a *gitano* boy named Jesús. What was he doing now? Certainly not living it up at a gala ball. "The most effective fake is produced by white spinel, a stone grown from seed crystal dipped in and then gradually withdrawn from a number of minerals. One is simulating nature's process over a million years in a matter of months. But, of course, no matter how well it is cut it can not match the fire of the real thing."

I was still interviewing the Amsterdam wholesaler, when Max joined us, glass in hand, speech a little slurred, determined to out-expert the experts. "Don't you think strontium titanate provides a better reflective surface?" he asked. "Anyhow, whatever the fakers use, I pride myself I can spot the real thing a mile off."

The wholesaler, in words more polite than mine, invited Max to put his money where his mouth was: and before I could see the way the situation was developing, Max had wagered a couple of hundred thousand pesetas on his professional skill. Several of the conference delegates were getting in on the act like boisterous puppy dogs. I had to admit to myself it would make compulsive listening.

"What is that tiara?" a delegate asked, pointing to a swept-up blonde floating by in an Italian's arms.

"Almost certainly a natural rock crystal, but not a crystalline form of carbon. In other words, gentlemen, not the real thing." Max was enjoying himself immensely. "But that little lady sitting over there is quite definitely wearing the real thing."

A dozen, or more, male eyes focused on the little lady. And on the butch dyke sitting with her.

"A tiara possibly, but not a pair of small ear-rings, not from this distance," the wholesaler was saying.

The black jacketed men were walking across the dance floor like the mob in an old gangster movie.

"You don't know what you're doing," I hissed at Max.

"On the contrary, old man," he said, *sotto voce*. "They're the pair I purchased for our mutual friend, John Truscott. Worth every bit of ten thousand smackers. She's a lucky little lady."

"She's not lucky, you fool. Don't you realize they're in love!"

When we reached the table, Pippa was aware something dreadful was about to happen to her. There was fear in her eyes as she reached out to hold Mari-Carmen's arm.

"Would you mind very much if I took a closer look at these lovely ear-rings you are wearing?" Max was asking.

I saw Pippa's complexion blanch under the cosmetic, as she tried to force a smile to disguise her shaking hand. Mari-Carmen was muttering, "Paste,paste. They're not real. How *could* they be real?" And there was Max, eye-glass screwed in his right eye, peering at the carbon fire in his left hand. I shall never forget the tune the band was playing at the time. *Diamonds Are a Girl's Best Friend.*

"They're beautifully set, my dear." Max handed the ear-ring back to the trembling Pippa. "But I'm afraid they're not real diamonds. Very lovely. Like you. But not real."

I called a waiter to replenish the girls' champagne. They really needed it. A little distance away I saw Max writing a cheque for the Amsterdam wholesaler. I felt more than a little sorry for the man. He had lost more than money, he had lost his professional pride. I think he blamed me for the turn of events. He was booked on an early morning flight to London and made this his excuse for an instant departure. His last, bitter words to me were: "Behind the bike shed at school – you always did mix it!"

I left the high-jinks myself at about four with half a dozen usable interviews and rather fewer pleasant memories; but away from the intoxication of the crowd, my conscience was nagging me. I began the day telling myself that I was in no way responsible for the well being of a *gitano* boy named Jesús: I ended it by falling into a fretful sleep, convinced that whatever had happened to him was in some way because of me. Then, to compound my confusion, I had a nightmare that left my bed linen wet with perspiration. I dreamt that my dead lover, Paul, was my judge, which was sick for a start. Anyone who knew Paul, knew his loathing of G and S comic operas, and *Trial by Jury* in particular. Yet there he was, telling the world that he was a judge and a good judge, too, while somewhere on the fringe was old Don Luis in moth-eaten wig, holding back what seemed to be a limitless crowd scene of *gitano* extras, all accusing me of breech of promise. 'But I haven't promised anything,' I protested as the verbal accusations materialised into heavy, leaden letters, hurled at me, tearing me to pieces, dragging me down. 'Fraud!' 'Cheat!' 'Liar!' 'Queer!'

It was nearly midday before I'd washed and shaved, forced myself to squeeze some oranges, and grabbed a cab to get me to Don Luis's chambers. "I've had my apartment wrecked by the police," I told him. "And they've as good as told me I'm to be prosecuted for handling dangerous drugs passed on to me by a *gitano* youth who, as far as I know is too young to shave, let alone deal in dangerous drugs."

"Let's set out the facts first and then we can get a clear picture of the situation." The old man's total calm was the therapy I needed. When he saw I was no longer in a state of frightened confusion, he said: "First, I must have access to this young man, to find out what he has to say for himself. How well to you know him?"

"I don't know him at all."

"And you expect me to believe that?"

"It's the truth," I insisted.

"Do you know his name?" When I mentioned Heredias the old man's demeanour dramatically changed. "Heredias. Now that to a *gitano* is like royalty to the English landed gentry."

"In what way? Any more for polo?"

"Don Manuel Heredias, a Spanish industrialist, opened an iron ore mine and smelting works near Marbella in the 1880s. You can still see the remains of the loading piers today. It was only the *gitanos* who could cope with the intense heat; but the Spanish gentry so hated them because they had no civil status – "

"They still hate them," I interrupted.

"The law was on the side of the landed gentry – and it remains that way today. Consequently, the *gitanos* were rounded up by the mounted *carabineros* and deported. In order to protect his workers, Don Manuel went to the civil governor, together with a lawyer and a priest, and he and his wife legally adopted every single *gitano* working for them, the priest baptizing them so that 'each and every one will be incorporated into society as the children of God that they are, and as our adopted sons." There were tears in the old lawyer's eyes when he finished telling me the story.

"Now wild horses won't stop me getting to know the young man, whatever he may have done," I told Don Luis.

In little more than an hour, Don Luis had seen a friend in the civil governor's office and we had a permit to visit the remand prisoner in Carranque, a bleak complex of cement monotony whose inmates were mostly allowed out to sweep roads by day, returning to their cells at night. Jesús was like a frightened animal, cowering on a stool in a corner of his cell. I discovered later that he had never been in a room alone before, nor had he been made to sleep alone in hostile surroundings.

When he recognized me, he managed a flicker of a smile. He was wearing the same green shirt I saw him wearing at Easter. I could see now it was several sizes too big for him, for under his clothes was an under-developed body that needed to flesh out. What struck me about him at once, was the direct and open way he looked me straight in the eyes.

"That piece of paper with my address on it, the police think you're dealing in drugs and I'm implicated in some way."

The eyes remained open, fixed on mine. "I swear by all that's holy, *señor*, I know nothing of drugs."

"What is holy to you?" Don Luis asked.

There was not the slightest hesitation. "My papa. He taught me all I know. And my mamma. She gave me life."

Don Luis turned to me. "He's a Heredias all right. Now,

let's see about getting him out of here."

In all my life, I've never known an old man work so hard, or so quickly, as Don Luis. We adjourned to a cafeteria opposite the prison where the faded, food stained menus still repeated the classic 'rape, the sailor's way' translation *gaffe* of the Franco era, and while I searched for more abuses of our mother tongue and tried not to offend the *patron* by forcing myself to drink his over-brewed coffee, Don Luis must have put through more than thirty phone calls in as many minutes. As I tried to keep up with him on the return canter to the prison cells, I noticed he'd left his coffee untouched.

"Would you be prepared to live in the Englishman's apartment?" the wise old bird asked the frightened youngster. "Do the housework for him? Do exactly what you are told? If you agree, I know a judge who may get you out of here, and we can take our time making sure there are no reasons for you to be brought back. So, what's it to be?"

"Oh yes, yes, yes," the youngster gasped.

"Then I'11 contact your papa and mamma and let them know what we have in mind for you. By this time tomorrow you'll be having your first English lesson."

Jesús wept.

A LEAP OVER THE HEDGE . . .

(Cervantes)

I SAW THE DOBERMANN streaking along the sidewalk from my window, J.C. just about on his feet at the other end of the leash. They barely made the loo in time to throw up. I'd been sitting on the throne myself for the best part of the morning and was running a temperature, no fit condition to host my Radio Independiente Plus show the following day.

"It must have been the fish," Jesús said, when he had finished emptying himself both ends. He'd only been released by the authorities a couple of weeks. He was determined to earn his independence, of me (in particular) and the world (in general). So he started the dog-walk service for the neighbourhood apartment dwellers, though the larger breeds walked him.

When the doctor called, he diagnosed ptomaine poisoning and prescribed suppositories. The Spanish have a penchant for them that can only have some Freudian significance. My first encounter with them, many years ago when I had 'flu, ended by my trying to stuff them up my nose. J.C. was convulsed by this story. "We'll have to stuff them up Julio next time he calls. He sold us the stinking fish."

I hated to think it of Julio; he'd been selling me fresh fish for years, and the suspect *besugo* had looked clean enough round the gills. Caught that morning, he assured me, by him and his dad in their boat off E1 Palo.

The last thing I wanted was for the probation officer or, worse, J.C.'s mum to think I was poisoning my charge. As it was the doctor, who I'd never seen in my life before, asked with tactless normality who'd cooked for us. Getting a house call in Spain is no easy matter. The insurance company excelled itself by sending a genuine Brit who knew all the ingredients of the drugs he could dispense, but was incapable of getting into his head the idea that men may be better cooks than women. He was picking up his little black bag to depart as Don Luis arrived with the news that J.C.'s movements were no longer to be restricted.

"You can leave the city any time you wish," he said. "So long as you have your employer's permission to do so."

The sorting out of Jesús's life had proved more difficult than the old lawyer had anticipated. We discovered somewhat late in the day that he was the victim of a classic police balls-up. Several hundred officers had been drafted into Málaga capital for Semana Santa and one of them, a *cabo* based in Ronda, grabbed an opportunity for promotion when he saw half a dozen youths in an alley near the Aduana mixing Moroccan cannabis resin. In their flight, they rid themselves of the evidence on J.C.'s stall of crosses and crucifixes: and J.C., having exceptional confidence in the integrity of the Policia Nacional, almost to the point of gullibility, didn't for a moment think the night court judge would take the dishonest word of one Ronda policeman of many years corruption against the honest word of an Andalusian *gitano* of some fewer years innocence. Of the night court judge, Don Luis said he was a man of few morals and much learning, and the Ronda *cabo*, a man of many morals and little learning: between them, J.C. didn't stand a chance of a fair hearing. Don Luis's ploy had been an appeal at which Jesús pleaded guilty to having the cannabis on his stall, but not guilty to dealing, or possession. It was enough to get him off the hook with a court order of eighteen months social services supervision: and the Ronda *cabo* still had his chance for promotion.

"Would you like me to clean the *motor* this afternoon, Mister Peter?" Jesús asked.

I knew why he'd asked. I'd promised to take him pillion along the Costa as soon as the court granted him freedom of movement. "Fine. But no strings attached."

"Please, I don't understand. What strings?"

"It means, I can see right through you," I said. "So, watch it!"

"I still don't understand. How do you see through me?'

"And you can stop sending me up!"

"What is sending up?" For reply, he got the old two-finger sign: that, he did understand.

While J.C. cleaned my pride-and-joy I sat in the shade in the park with a clipboard, editing a couple of tape transcripts and watching through the exotic plants to where the sailors were coming ashore from two Spanish ships that had just berthed in the harbour. They had gone into white for the summer and, like boisterous puppy-dogs, were making their *piropos* (a kind of verbal bottom-pinching) to every *chica* that passed, from nine to ninety, whether or not accompanied by a matronly mum. *'Vaya Ud. con Dios señora, y su hija conmigo'*. (Go with God, Madam, but your daughter comes with me). How marvellous to be a woman! I'd scatter the lot of them like blushing schoolboys, just by pinching the nearest bell-bottom right back and shouting for all to hear: "Who's first into the bushes?" But women didn't think like that, even lesbian women like my producer didn't seem to think like that. I was watching an exceptionally fair-haired young sailor being cruised by a macho business executive, who was kerb-crawling in an Alfa-Romero; and it suddenly dawned on me, the extent to that which polite society likes to call sexual deviation, unites black and white, rich and poor, political left and right, the religious and the agnostic. As Paul always used to say, being gay is like being a member of the best club in the world.

I returned to the apartment in time to help my neighbours, the two thick ladies, depart with their cross for Lourdes. They were travelling by long-distance coach, which was equipped to take Rafael and his wheel-chair, but it was a gruelling thirty-six hour journey none the less; and as J.C. pushed the wheel-chair and I carried the heavy luggage across the city centre to the bus station, I was fearful I might inadvertently betray my lack of enthusiasm for a gamble I knew was costing them more than just the money they could ill afford to spend.

"When you come back," Jesús told Rafael, "we can go swimming together in Torremolinos."

"Rafael may not like swimming," I said obliquely.

"Then I'll take him to Mijas to ride the *burro* taxis."

"I suggest you don't count chicken before they're

hatched, young man," I told him. I'd have a lot more to tell him when I got him home.

"What does that mean, Mister Peter?" Jesús asked disarmingly.

"It means, I'm going to give you a lesson in English proverbs. Pronto." I'd thought at first that J.C.'s innocence was a bit overdone, a bit too calculated; but I was beginning to see that it wasn't so much innocence that he possessed as a purity of heart that provided a hard shell of protection against all the world could hurl at him.

The thick ladies insisted on us all having chocolate and *churros* – at the bus station, of all places. They were awful, and made me late for a dinner date with Mari-Carmen, which I assumed was to be in her apartment. But when I pressed the button of the video security-porter to announce my arrival, a big close-up of what appeared to be Mari-Carmen's right nostril came on the screen, accompanied by a voice so distorted it took what seemed like half an hour to get *her* (and not *me*) positioned for camera, light and sound – by which time two unchecked security risks had gained entry to the building. Eventually, I was told not to come up but to wait. I'd been waiting another half hour when a Policia Municipal car screeched to a halt and I found myself surrounded with demands to know why I was *'holgazanear'*, *'merodear'*, and other words with which I was not familiar. To compound the situation I'd left my passport in the jeans I had been wearing earlier in the day. I was being invited, politely enough, to wait for Mari-Carmen at the cop-shop, when she appeared, crammed into undersize black tights, a black floppy blouse bejewelled in oversize crap, and her face streaked with hastily applied liquid make-up.

"Why have you called the *policia*, Pedro? " she demanded.

"*I* haven't called them! They've called *us*!"

The apartments were small, modern and ugly, trumpeted by the estate agents as the *ultimas viviendas*, and just about affordable on Mari-Carmen's salary, if I am any judge of what she can squeeze out of Tio Mac.

"I want you to meet some English neighbours of mine," she said. "Their apartment is there – " She pointed with a gloved finger, then suddenly snatched it back, examining it as though it was under a microscope. "I wear too much black, no?" She gave me a defensive little grin.

"No," I said, rapidly changing the subject. "Torre del Mar is the up and coming resort now, isn't it?"

"There's no more land west, so we're having to build east. Spain will be a wonderful country when they've finished it." She had to have the last word. "And I do wear too much black."

She'd landed us both on an elderly couple, the Penroses, newly retired from England, who'd taken the penthouse.In reality it was little more than a shack next to the lift engine-house, but it did have a view inland towards Velez and the Sierra de Loja. Mr Penrose was a clock-maker, more than capable of holding his own on the Costa to judge by the alacrity with which he placed business cards in our hands, the nomenclature 'Horology' featuring prominently in red. Mari-Carmen was about to ask for a reading, but I saw the clanger coming and silenced her in time. Time, indeed, was everywhere; the apartment was full of singing, striking, chiming, music-playing timepieces, all of Mr Penrose's own design. It was for these the dinner party was being given, for Mari-Carmen had promised to produce a nice young English broadcaster (me), who would interview them (the clocks), for her programme. I made it quite clear to our hosts that I was not *that* young, that I had no experience interviewing clocks, and it was my show and not hers.

"We're doing our best to learn the lingo," Mr Penrose said, "but it's not easy for an old dog to learn new tricks. I don't know what we'd have done without Mari-Carmen's help."

I gathered they had barely survived their baptism of fire. First the water that only ran from the taps three or four hours a day, the electricity that surged and blew light bulbs every night, the unexpected demands for money – for the boy who cleaned the swimming pool and turned out to be the concierge's son – the noise of unsilenced mopeds and the barking of neighbourhood dogs. The list seemed endless. I was wondering how a couple of Spanish pensioners would fare in England, making a retirement home in Worthing, when Mr Penrose said: "I don't know how my wife would cope without Leticia. When Mari-Carmen found her for us, we didn't know what a godsend she would be."

I looked carefully at the messenger from the Deity. The crow's feet round the eyes never moved as she feasted off the pert little housemaid, who was scurrying between kitchen and living room, preparing the table for the meal. It was sadly evident that Mrs Penrose had yet to acquire the knack of using Spanish ingredients. I chewed my way through a beef casserole, fearful of washing it down with too much rough wine, trying to keep an intelligent conversation going about clocks, while Mari-Carmen was doing her best to seduce Leticia with small talk. We finished the evening with a precious bottle of Scotch, which I hate, the more because I suspected this particular bottle represented the last surviving contact with the homeland. I promised I'd return in a few days time to record the Penrose clocks for my programme, and hastened to disentangle my producer from the god-sent Leticia before the Scotch, with which she was not familiar, caused her to behave in a manner all too familiar – and definitely not lady producer-like.

I escorted her the short distance to her apartment and, more out of curiosity than concern for her well being, asked, "Will Pippa be waiting up for you?"

"Pippa doesn't live with me," she said. "The family does, or rather, I live with them. We were in Capuchinos till they redeveloped the *rambla*." She hesitated, but went on. "You don't understand the difficulties we have in Spain, you being English."

"I think I do," I said.

The thought of going back to an empty apartment always filled me with an inexplicable fear; but few young Spaniards, straight or gay, can live together in their own place. Economic pressures, the need for large families to be sustained, often on the earning of only one bread-winner, either delay marriage till in some cases middle age has set the mould, or the newly weds must set up home in the family house. My producer was no exception. So many young people have nowhere to make love unless they can afford to run a car, an essential feature of which must be the reclining front seats. In many families bed time must be scheduled and adolescent boys deprived their own den, deprived even a quiet place for a private wank. I am convinced one of the main reasons Spain has so many family-run taxis is the shortage of bed space: both car and bed operate three eight-hour shifts a day. They miss so much of life's deep joy. Little things, like the two tooth-brushes side by side in the bathroom, the two armchairs equidistant on either side of the TV, the two names side by side on the mailbox in the entrance hall. Love is shared memories: the bitterness of old age is the loneliness of having had no past to share. I'd had that past, with Paul. But lurking somewhere in my subconscious was the question: Could I now share a second past with a physically perfect, honest, obliging, clean, intelligent *gitano* so many years my junior?

The clean, intelligent *gitano* was riding pillion on the way back from Gib the following afternoon, the day-out I'd promised him. The Rock had failed to impress and he was more interested in our doing a ton along the deserted Costa road during siesta, so our day-out looked like becoming half a day-out. I'd slowed down as we approached the long, dusty road that runs parallel to the beach at Benalmadena, when the lion came crashing onto the parked Seat 'Panda' like manna out of heaven. I slammed the brakes on the Harley and nearly had J.C. over my shoulders. The lion was dazed by the fall. So was the little 'Panda', its roof buckled like a child's beach bucket. We looked up at the high-rise apartments. From somewhere near the top, two heads were peering over the balcony, one black, the other white, both shouting to us in a Babel of languages.

"He's quite tame . . . but he's not used to heights!" the white head shouted.

It was obvious from the blood on the beast's front paw that he was injured. Presently, the owner appeared on the sidewalk with only a towel wrapped round his naked body. He was about twenty-five, on the verge of being skinny, more pink than tanned and had sunken eyes which, combined with the long matted fair hair, left an impression he was wild, if not a little mad. I assumed he'd been having sex with his black jungle mate.

"His name's Leo," he said.

"That's original." I looked apprehensively at the wounded animal. "He needs proper attention after a fall like that."

J.C. said he knew a horse doctor some miles inland who looked after an uncle's *burros* when they got colic. I stupidly allowed him to charm a gullible taxi driver into accepting the fare, with the assurance that there was no difference between Leo and a domestic *gato*, except size. The owner, who was doing his best to look sultry but only succeeded in looking hot and bothered, removed his towel to stanch the flow of blood from the injured paw and, like Adam, suddenly aware of his nakedness, fled into the apartment doorway. And that was the start of my nightmare.

We returned to Benalmadena some three hours later with a bandaged lion which was showing every sign of feeling a little peckish, if not downright ravenous, paid the rapacious taxi driver ten thousand pesetas for his paramedic services, and set about returning Leo to . . . Tarzan? It only then occurred to me that I did not know the owner's name. We spent a frantic fifteen minutes pressing all the buttons on the security-porter and speaking to those that answered, none of whom knew a white owner of a tame lion nor the black owner of a wild white. I had a lion I didn't want and a houseboy about whom I was rapidly gathering like feelings. The next move was decided for me by the arrival of two municipal police officers, accompanied by the distraught owner of the battered 'Panda'. Not surprisingly, we all ended up in the local cop shop. I was held responsible for the damage done by the king of beasts till such a time I could prove other ownership: and Leo, doing little on his part to charm the boys in blue, was handed over to the near-by Safari Park for temporary board and lodging. I hoped their fees would not be as great as Leo's apparent appetite, if his now audibly rumbling tum-tum was anything to go by.

"All's well that ends well," Jesús said, as we resumed our ride home. I decided I'd taught the little bastard too much English. The all was just beginning.

The following day I rode out to Torre del Mar to record the Penrose clocks. Mrs Penrose had taken Leticia out with her on a shopping expeditions and the whole time we were making the recording I sensed there was something the old man wanted to talk to me about other than his clocks.

"We were both very grateful to your producer for finding the housemaid for us," he said at last. "Only – well, it hasn't been without its problems. I suppose we should mention it to Mari-Carmen, but she seems so attached to the girl."

"What sort of problems?" I asked. I hoped I wasn't about to become involved in another sordid layer of Mari-Carmen's private life. I was beginning to like the silly bitch.

"She seemed so cheerful when she first started. Always singing to herself. Now she's morose, seldom smiles and – well, she's started to steal things. Packets of food, small change from my wife's purse and what has upset Mrs Penrose very much, we're almost certain she's taken the gold powder compact given to my wife by the bowling club in recognition of her twenty-five years as secretary."

"But surely you've had it out with the girl?"

He looked as bemused as a small child. "It's difficult getting through to her, not knowing much of the language. Besides, she's so secretive. She won't even let us do anything about the unpleasant incident with the concierge a few days ago,"

Sex, I thought, was about to rear its ugly head. As usual, I was right.

"My wife and I were visiting friends in Fuengirola," Mr Penrose went on, "and my wife went back to get the address book she had forgotten. She found the concierge in the apartment, struggling with Leticia in our bedroom. The girl's clothes were – well, it was quite obvious to my wife the man was forcing his attentions on her."

What I enjoyed most about the titillation was the old world charm with which the story was told. "Someone should speak to the girl's parents," I said. "Before matters get worse."

The moment I'd said it, I wished I hadn't, for the old man was asking me to do the speaking. I've never spoken to a girl's parents in my life before, about anything, certainly not about attempted rape, petty larceny and other delicate areas of human communication. But Mari-Carmen is too attached, I heard Mr Penrose saying yet again, and I heard myself saying yes, she is too attached, too.

"I saw Julio this morning," Jesús said, as he began his demonstration of how to skin a rabbit. "No wonder we got fish poisoning. He was in the harbour, trying to freshen up fish he'd scavenged from the wholesale market. In the filthy bilge water at the end of the quay." The rabbit had been mysteriously left on our doorstep, J.C. thought by his 'country cousin' who couldn't read and therefore couldn't write a message either. But he was determined to finish putting the knife in Julio. "And Angel, the boy I was telling you about who works the copier in the justice department, says the law may be after him for whoring his arse in the park."

"Julio? I can't believe it." It wasn't the Julio I knew, courting his bosomly girl at my favourite *chiringuito* on the El Palo beach, where I eat grilled *sardinas* most summer Sunday mornings.

As it happened, Julio had the nerve to come hawking his fish later the same morning. I dragged him in and bolted the door. Short legs, long neck, the typical Mediterranean male, he stood there with his two buckets of fish hanging at either side from a rope slung across his shoulders Málaga-style. His hands were raised on the defensive, as though he was expecting physical attack.

"Are you aware we were as sick as pigs last time you called?" I bellowed. "I should kick you out of here!"

Instead, I took a bottle of beer from the refrigerator and sat him at the kitchen table. He declined a glass and drank nervously from the bottle. Gnarled hands but as yet beardless face, he was still the insecure adolescent, trapped between puberty and adultery.

"It won't happen again, *señor*, I promise," he said, trying to avoid me with his eyes.

"And will you go on whoring yourself in the park with those sad old men? What would your girl say if she knew?"

It was a sorry tale of economic disaster Julio had to tell. Sea pollution, combined with a government ban on fishing the much in demand *chanquetes* and little support from the European Union, had reduced the off-shore catch to starvation level. His dad had taken to drink as the easiest way out. Julio realized that the only way to support the family was to continue his hawking with fish from the wholesale market. But to buy his stock he needed money and –

"I went into the park. I hate those bloody queers, begging your pardon, *señor*." He drank anxiously from the bottle. "I tried taking out *extranjeros* sports fishing, but the way some of the men looked at me . . . I might have thrown one of them overboard."

I felt wretched for Julio, and all the other Julios trapped by ill fortune. I promised to do what I could to help, and we parted friends again.

We were about to eat the rabbit when radio Rip-Rip-Hurrah! (as J.C. insisted on calling it) put out my flying lion story. I had just found the red currant jelly, a Christmas gift from a distant relative back in the UK and was wondering if it would do anything for the rabbit that J.C.'s park-gathered rosemary hadn't already done, when the duty officer at the station put through a call from a female listener of indeterminate age who gushed at me about a nightery in Torremolinos, where a lion she thought was stuffed, licked her on a most delicate part of her anatomy and caused her to ruin an original Dior gown.

BOBO's looks, was, and is a clip joint; but it does the business because half of its punters are encouraged to get their kicks enjoying the sight of the other half getting clipped. Bobo operates a tricky balancing act when it comes to how much he should help the media in order to help himself. "Yes, we did have a lion in here a few days ago," he told me cautiously.

"Whose?" I studied the fat black face and wondered if it would be prepared to name names.

"Spence Church." He broke off to give some pallid youth a rocket for the dying flowers among the table posies. "There was a loud argument between him and a Senegalese woman. Church is from South Africa."

"And the argument was about?"

Bobo heaved his vast round shoulders. "Do I need to tell *you* how testy the South Africans still are in the matter of miscegenation?" He opened his hands expressively, then closed them tight as though to indicate the interview was over.

Bobo is an intellectual among night club operators: but I wouldn't tell this to his black face. A swollen head would make him completely unapproachable. Instead, I asked, "Where do I find the elusive Church?"

"I don't. You don't. No one don't. Is that clear?"

"Very," I said, and got the hell out of it before Bobo put me on his black list. Or worse.

The road back to the capital would take me near Leticia's home in the underprivileged Trinidad district. I tried to think of a reason for putting off my promised call, but in the end decided I'd have to go through with it. The confrontation proved even more gruelling than I had feared. What remained of the family lived in a geranium festooned *casa mata*. There was just the mother, and a young woman of about nineteen she called Teresa, confined to a wheel-chair and unable to speak since being run down by a car five years previously; and Leticia. The father, I gathered, had died of lung cancer some three years ago and, having plied what little skill he had odd-jobbing in the flourishing black economy, his name appeared on no official list; so that what remained of the family had no official list to which they could appeal to supplement their income. As I hoped, Leticia was still at work. The matter was delicate enough without her being there; but I had completely miscalculated the mother's reaction.

"If Leticia has misbehaved, you must speak to her about it, not me," she said, with undisguised hostility. "It's all I can do to earn enough to look after Teresa and myself."

Suddenly, I knew where I'd seen the woman before. She was one of Radio Independiente's cleaners, which explained how Mari-Carmen came to be pimping the daughter to the Penroses. "Leticia may lose her job if she doesn't mend her ways," I said.

"Then she'll have to lose it. She's out of my control." There was an air of utter resignation in the voice.

"Aren't you even concerned that the concierge where she works may have sexually assaulted her?"

"No harm can come to my Leticia. She knows how to look after herself. Thank you for calling; but now, will you please leave?"

And that was it. That was all the mother love I got out of the woman. I had to admit defeat. I told myself the whole matter wasn't any concern of mine. Next time I saw Mari-Carmen I'd alert her to what was going on, and leave it to her to sort out her neighbours' problems.

The following day I overslept, so it was nearly midday before I saw the headlines in *Sur*. There had been panic in a Fuengirola swimming pool when some *tonto* had taken the plunge together with his pet alligator. For the first time in years, I left the apartment unshaven. The pool was part of a motel and rent-a-villa complex. Spence had paid a month's rent in advance, but when it was opened up for me, apart from a strong smell of fish, the only sign of habitation was the grinning reptile in the bath. As I was the only contact the management had with the zany South African, I was promptly made responsible for the damned thing. It didn't seem to like me. The feeling was mutual.

"The early bird catches the worm," was all the sympathy I got from J.C. when I told him what had happened.

"And here's one for you, if you must converse in proverbs. Absence makes the heart grow fonder."

We weren't talking for the rest of the day. I went out for an early evening drink to one of my favourite bodegas and Manolo, who runs the Slipped Disc and who shares my taste in most things, was just leaving. He'd been buying drinks all round to judge by the chalk marks on the bar, and mixed up with a handful of coins was a lady's gold compact.

"I'm not going limp-wrist," he grinned, seeing my quizzical glance. "One of the kid's dropped it at our drag queen contest last night. I shoved it in my pocket and I've been carrying it around with me all day. It must be his mother's . . . something about twenty-five years as secretary . . . "

"Let me see it!" I virtually snatched it from him. The name was quite clearly engraved: LAURA PENROSE. "Sorry to tell you, Manny, but this is stolen property."

"How do you know?" Manolo asked anxiously. His place has been in trouble with the authorities more than enough.

"I happen to know the owner. And very soon I will know the little bastard who stole it, if I can look through your contest entry forms."

"Anything. Any time. You know that." Sweat was pouring off his forehead. "Little things like this stick in the official mind and that's the last thing I want just now."

I'd confused Thursday with Friday, and if J.C. hadn't come into my room and woken me with a tumbler of cool, freshly made orange juice, I would have failed to make the bus station in time to meet the two thick ladies returning with their cross from their pilgrimage to Lourdes. A grey dawn was being tinted pink in the east, as the long-distance coach pulled into its bay. A sad assortment of travel-weary invalids and their carers descended, and waited patiently for the two drivers to hustle tips before handing out the heavy luggage.

"Did it all go as you expected?" I asked the mother, careful to avoid emotive words such as 'success', 'cure', and above all, 'miracle'.

"Father Carnicero, our officially appointed tour guide,

gave us all a lot of encouragement," the mother said. "These things take time. But we have a lot of good men praying for us."

Rafael appeared to be sleeping; but a slight blueness about the face suggested a massive sedation. "He looks contented," I said, "You must all be exhausted. We thought you'd be more comfortable having your usual *desayuno* back at the apartment, so Jesús has fixed it."

The aunt beamed. "He's such a good boy." I thought she was going to add, 'for a *gitano*', but she didn't.

"He's been doped!" Jesús said, ignoring the compliment and shaking Rafael's shoulder as he lolled in his wheel-chair.

"Only what the doctor prescribes for him," the mother said defensively.

"And is the doctor one of the good men praying for him?" There was an anger in J.C.'s eyes I had not seen before.

At that moment, I wished I had never found Jesús. I said, to excuse him, "J.C.'s a bit anti-doctors right now. We both are since our fishy-dishy a while back." But the damage had been done. The home-coming was far from a triumphant success.

A couple of hours later I was on the air, trying to camp up a piece about Ali the alligator, who had now been added to my menagerie at the Safari Park, when a Mijas woman rang to say she'd just seen a big snake eat her prize Pomeranian. There was instant dispute in the studio as to whether a Pomeranian was pooch, plant or person. While Mari-Carmen was doing battle with our balance engineer, I slipped out and, with my pride-and-joy between my legs, headed into the *montes*. Screw the listeners! I knew damn well that when Mari-Carmen realized I wasn't there, she'd lose no time putting her atrocious accent to work D-jaying the rest of my morning discs. Mijas is a wholly delightful little *pueblo* in the foothills, a few miles inland from the less delightful part of the Costa. These days it has virtually been taken over by *extranjeros*, who do not expect dog-eating snakes to be indigenous. This time I was in luck. The elusive Spence Church was living in a self-catering apartment over a harness-maker, whose brightly coloured craft for use by the *burro* taxis was displayed outside.

"Go away! Go away! This is private property. You have no right to be here."

I'd caught up with Tarzan at last and he was no great jungle specimen. I told him he owed me and I intended to collect. Then I saw the snake in the corner. It was coiled up with a bulge, which I took to be the hapless Pomeranian, some twelve inches from its mouth. I was mesmerised by the thing.

"Do you like animals?" the man was asking.

"Animals, yes. But this is a monster! Have you any idea of how much you've cost me?"

"Write it down on a piece of paper with your address and leave it face down on the table. Then I'll have a guess. If I guess right, we'll call it quits. Otherwise I'll get them to put a certified cheque in the post."

"No thanks." I'd had enough of writing my name and address on scraps of paper for one lifetime. "Who are them, Mr Church?"

"My bankers, my chief accountant, my secretary . . . good grief, man, don't you trust me?"

"Frankly, no." It took me some minutes to realize the man was actually crying.

"What is it you want?" He sounded all in. "Tell me the amount and I'll have it cabled here while you wait."

I made a rapid calculation of my expenses and doubled them. "Quarter of a million," I said.

"Quarter of a million what? Pesetas, pounds, dollars, yen?" He was quite mad: or I was.

"Pesetas," my far from easy conscience muttered.

He picked up a phone and dialled a few numbers and almost instantly began talking to someone in South Africa. "It'll be with us in a few minutes. But promise me one thing."

"Tell me the one thing first", I said cautiously.

He was desperate to talk. To anyone. About how he fell

in love with his black mate, how they'd had a child that her sister was keeping safe in Senegal, and how his father had sworn to kill him for so dishonouring the family name. "I dare not stay in one place more than a few days, hours even, at a time," he said. "Promise to stop broadcasting my movements. Please!"

"I suggest you lead a more normal life, petwise," I told him. "That at least should solve your logistic problem."

I've met some strange people on the Costa, but Spence Church was unique. I still think the Banco Central clerk, who delivered the certified cheque by hand, was a ghost; but the cheque was real enough. All the same, I was glad to get out into the bright sunlight.

I paused in the land of the living to say *hasta luego* to the harness-maker. "Are you the oldest man in the *pueblo*?" I asked.

"No, *señor*, we haven't got one," he wheezed. "He died last year."

I collected the drag queen entry forms from Manolo that evening. There were more than a hundred of them. I had no idea there were so many Málaga youngsters anxious to camp it up. My eyes scanned the names and addresses. One immediately caught my attention. It was a geranium festooned *casa mata* in Trinidad, where lived a Miguel I knew nothing about. Yet.

When her peasant instinct alerted her to the purpose of my second visit, the mother was far less hostile. "I didn't know he was stealing," she said. "I knew he had to dress up. I thought that was all part of the job, like waiters have to dress up."

"Are we talking about a boy, or a girl?" I asked. "Or a transvestite?"

"He's a boy!" she said, with genuine pride in her voice. "And he works hard for Teresa and me!"

Teresa was seated at the table, silent, her eyes following my every movement. I had a frightening thought. Together, these two women would kill me if it would protect what remained of their family. "I'm pleased to hear that," I said.

"Many a fine gentleman has promised to do things for

Miguel, but nothing ever comes of it. Just promises, promises, promises."

I waited for Miguel at the Torre del Mar bus stop and caught him, or rather I caught Leticia on her way home from work. He/she went a deathly pale when he knew I knew.

"I'm not having a little shit like you upset two elderly folk who deserve better," I told him/her. "I'm giving you a chance. You return the presentation compact to Mrs Penrose . . . and if she forgives you, its more than you deserve."

"I couldn't. Not in drag."

"You got the job in drag. You keep it in drag!"

"I'd be too ashamed . . . "

"I know just the person to give you moral support," I told him. "Be outside Radio Independiente tomorrow, at noon."

Mari-Carmen thought *her* programme was shaping up nicely. She was particularly pleased with her item on the Penrose clocks. I agreed that in the best of possible worlds she was the best of possible producers.

"Leticia wants to make amends. I said you'd give her moral support."

The war-paint fairly cracked at the prospect of getting a little more firmly attached to her protégé. Outside, on the sun drenched street, a couple of sailors were making their *piropos* to the pert little housemaid. Mari-Carmen shooed them angrily away. Leticia was all hers. She was like a fox set to guard the chicken coop as I helped her bundle the youngster into her tiny red Seat.

" Bye-bye, Mari-Carmen! Have fun!" I knew it was wicked of me to be doing such a thing, but I just couldn't resist it. The silly dyke was in for a helluva surprise siesta!

It was a sultry afternoon. The smoked pork chops my butcher brings in from the country once a month – when those in work have money to spend – were playing havoc with my digestion. I was only half asleep, or, put the other way, I was only half awake, alert enough to feel the griping pains of approaching old age. Reality fused with fantasy, so that I knew a big snake was doing its best to digest the two thick ladies, and Mari-Carmen, in hard hat and jeans, had a hard-on that needed a third man to help ease. I was trying to coax a drag queen to get in on the act, when the pain struck. Yeooooo! My gut was not just rumbling, it really hurts . . . .

The banging on the door was followed by the mother's urgent voice, "Come, please! At once!"

I thought a fire had broken out. I'm expecting one at any moment in some of Málaga's over-crowded under-protected older houses. What I was not expecting was the sight that confronted me in my neighbour's apartment. Rafael was in his room, naked except for his boxer shorts, laying face down over a stool and waving his arms and legs, looking for all the world like a stranded turtle. Standing over him was J.C., more naked than the other youth as J.C. wears the smallest of slips, so small that I had already pointed out to him they were not large enough to contain all his male bits and pieces. Rafael's aunt was running about the room like a chicken without its head, gathering up various items of discarded male clothing.

"One. Two. Three. Four." Jesús intoned, as he conducted Rafael's leg and arm movements.

"What the hell's going on here?" I demanded, trying to shake the sleep from my eyes.

"Raf *does* want me to take him swimming in Torremolinos," Jesús said.

"You're killing him! You're killing him! You wicked, wicked boy," the mother cried.

"How did you get him out of his wheel-chair?" I asked.

"He got out himself. He wanted to get out," Jesús said. "For me."

"You should have stayed in prison," the aunt shouted. "All you *gitanos* should be locked up!"

"Pray for him! Pray for him!" the mother was wailing. "Pray for him!"

Jesús was standing in the centre of the shaded room. Shafts of late afternoon sunlight flashed through the broken shutters to radiate his body. "In the words of Miguel Cervantes, great Spanish writer," he said. "A leap over the hedge is better than good men's prayers."

JUERGA

J.C.'s DAD TOOK one look at the reproduction of Don Luis's Picasso which hung over his son's bed and decided he wouldn't want the original even if it turned up in a hundred-pesetas shop. His mother, who was much larger both in sight and sound than I remembered her at police headquarters and the remand prison at Carranque, thought it was clever but not very *jondo*, not very *simpatico*: in spite of her bigness, Dolores le Grande was finding it difficult to be other than an ordinary, albeit *gitano* mum, confronted by the realities of life among we amoral Christians.

"At least I get my money when I sing," she said, "No one else gets it when I'm dead." She snapped out of her bitter mood with a display of *pitos* and an old trooper's smile. "A *copa* of fino to lubricate the tubes and I'll be ready."

J.C. had landed me with a full scale *juerga*. He'd said that as he was living with me it would be 'proper' to invite his family round for a drink; but this wasn't a family, it was a tribe. I had to yell above the hubbub that the neighbours would object if they insisted on bringing the assortment of hunting, guard and racing dogs, seven in all, into the apartment. Obviously, it was not going to be an evening of polite social drinking. Already the heady smell of brandy, anise, and *fino* was creating a massive ambience, and the singing and dancing had not yet begun. Two young women were helping the grandfather out of a much-travelled *caracol*, which he owned but which was driven by an uncle, on account of gramps not owning a driving licence to go with it. While they were hitching it to a lamp-post next to my Harley, I saw the municipal police descending. I fingered the bank-notes in my pocket as they invited themselves in, I hoped only for a drink, but I was to be proved wrong. Cousins, aunts, hangers-on, all were there, including the mysterious boy only seen at *feria* times, who played a bugle for a performing goat and claimed he'd run away from the Foreign Legion. One of the uncles who'd begun warming up his guitar told the mysterious one that a bugle was no fit instrument for the house. I was grateful the boy hadn't brought the performing goat, which wasn't fit for the house either. And there was Diego.

"Show them the poster, Diego!" Jesús said.

He was a thin, shy youth with large, watery eyes and long bony fingers that gave him the fragile appearance of a bird. His complexion was such that even one of purest Romany blood would have to admit he was born with a touch of the tar brush.

"It's my first fight, *señor,* " Diego said, as he fluttered with the bullfight poster.

I thought at first it was one of those colourful matador illustrations with the blank space for the tourist's name to be filled-in, but I just glimpsed the DIE- before it was swept to one side by the guitar-playing uncle and J.C.'s *flamenco*-singing mum as they began testing the acoustics of my living room which, having more tiles than the average English public loo, they declared to be perfect for their purpose. And so the *juerga* got under way, the heavy bosoms of the singer shaking her whole body till rustling layers of starched petticoats rode up to reveal brown, mosquito-bitten legs and swollen ankles. To the cries of '*Olé!*', the hard, clear voice began to fall in that sad cadence that tears out the Spanish soul and displays its bleeding roots for all to see. I realized at that moment how difficult it was for a *gitano* to painfully drag himself, or herself, out of that limbo in which society forces them to exist. Fighting bulls was one way. Singing was another. Education was a third. Jesús's mother earned sufficient to maintain a little house for her family in Alora, the fruit-picking centre of the province. She had given her only child a good education by local standards, but not good enough to keep him out of trouble with the law. And why, I asked myself, was he like his holy namesake, an only child? Had there been others? It was common knowledge that many *gitano* fathers made sure only male offspring survived. Tonight was filled with more than strange sounds. A whole new dimension of living was being thrust upon me. Some twelve hours later, after more bottles of *fino* than I could count, more *jamon serrano* than I could digest, and more bank-notes to vanish parking fines than I could afford, I was aware that J.C.'s dad was singing. To me. A *buleria* in my honour. The *payo* in their midst, he was singing, was a blood brother because he understood that ambitions were the enemy of freedom but principles were freedom's friend. The father's song was directed now to J.C. and his friend, Diego.

> *'*Maldita sea la cárcel, sepultura de hombres vivos,*
> *donde se amansan los guapos y se pierden los amigos.*'

My emotions got the better of me and I turned to look out of the window while I dried my tears. In the street below, the grandfather was giving the dogs water from my cracked Victorian po, which Paul and I used for making *sangria* when we threw camp parties. Together. The thought of Paul started me crying again. And then, as the guests were departing, J.C.'s mum made us a parting gift of a patchwork bed-cover she had made herself. It was for a double bed.

"You do not like my family, Mister Peter," Jesús said, seeing my red eyes. "They are not important people, like the people you know. They are little people, but they offer you their souls."

The grandfather and his driver were the last to leave, unhitching the priceless three-wheeler like a *burro*, dogs and old man piling into the rear in an overload of happy flesh. Foreigners often get the impression that the Spanish ill treat their animals. Nothing could be further from the truth. In some country areas, where poverty is endemic, you will see animals better fed than the people. An animal may be killed for food, reared for work, or kept to give pleasure: whatever its purpose, it is never deprived of its dignity. Even the fighting bull, bred for that one moment of truth at five in the afternoon, has a name, and is

---

*Damned be the jail, tomb of live men,
where spirits are tamed and friends are lost.

remembered by it, more often for longer than the matador is remembered, whose sword and cape can bring forth a noble epic, or merely a bloody mess.

A LAS CINCO DE LA TARDE *(Lorca)*

"YOU DID GIVE CANDY the tickets?" Diego was asking.

The dark glasses were doing little for my hangover, as I stood in the midday sun high up in a gallery of the Plaza de Toros, looking down into the corral where lots were being drawn for the six bulls to be fought that afternoon.

"Yes, I gave them to Candy," I said, barely able to hide my irritation.

How a street-wise youth like this could be so innocent was beyond me. He'd found himself in prison for hitting a Guardia Civil officer with a wine bottle he'd grabbed from a newspaper critic, done, Jesús insisted, in the heat of the moment. For a *maletilla* like Diego, drifting from town to town with wooden sword and small bundle of possessions, arrest was the logical consequence of leaping into the bullring to show his bravery. But on previous occasions he had not got involved in violence against one of the men in shiny bicorn hats.

"And you did tell Candy I'll return the money, just as soon as I'm famous?" the youngster asked in the same anxious voice.

"Yes, yes, yes," I said. I was far from grateful to my houseboy for getting me involved in an emotionally charged situation that could blow up in my face at any moment.

"Diego's second bull looks real mean," Jesús said. "See the way that right horn is twisted!"

Not half as twisted as Candy Floss, I thought. Diego had met Candy by fortuitous accident. Released from prison, he'd been found a job sweeping roads. Candy, the latest gender-bending pop sensation, born Andy Foss, aged twenty-two, son of a Blackpool rock purveyor, had been sitting at a sidewalk café sipping a coke when he saw a friend on the other side of the road. Candy, running to make contact, like all Brits looked right instead of left and would have made contact with a passing cement lorry had Diego not dragged him clear of the advancing horns.

Instead, they both landed under the hoofs of a brightly coloured horse-drawn carriage, overflowing with horrified tourists. The consequence was that both Diego and Candy were hospitalized: and Candy, learning that Diego needed money to buy his way into the bullfight business, the moment they were discharged took him on his first ever visit to a bank. A quarter of a million pesetas was a fortune to a boy like Diego; but to Candy it was a pittance, a minor feel-good offering to some one, or some thing, in a great flood of relief that injury would not bring about the cancellation of the up-coming tour of the U.S. of A. How could I tell Diego that Candy had already forgotten the money, had already forgotten him?

I'd gone to the Villa Mimosa, about the mostest for any hostess on the Marbella golden-mile with its hard and soft tennis courts, hot and cold pools, wet and dry sweat cabins, high-fi and low lights, which the Candy entourage had taken over for the season, in order to tape a day-in-the-life-of for my RIP show. At midday, Candy was just rising: a bleary-eyed white skeleton, blotched by too much *sol español* and a crop of body acne that twinkled under a masseur's firm touch. So this was what the perpetrator of *Send No Wreaths for a Well Hung Man* looked like divested of the personality of fashion.

"Diego asked me to give you these." I put the fight tickets on the bedside table and began setting up my recorder.

"Who's Diego?"

"You should know. You shared a room with him in the Carlos Haya clinic."

Candy reached for a bottle and swallowed a handful of pills. "Oh, that fruitcake! The one who prefers bulls to boys."

"I don't think sex means much to him yet," I said.

"It never will. He's hung like a hamster and it's not everyone who wants to be tickled to death."

I started the recorder and we talked about the much publicized Candy gender-bending make-up, the masculine hats and the feminine gowns that were a part of his act.

What was it like, I asked, knowing that half the audience thought he was a girl.

He stood by the dressing table, shaking scarlet varnish dry on his fingernails. "Jesús Christ was a limp-wrist," he said. "It was the nails that did it!"

The hotel by the *rambla* was shaded by palm trees, its rooms grouped around a blue-tiled patio from whence came the gentle plopping sound of water. The long white curtains occasionally stirred, letting flashes of sunlight steal into the dark interiors. J.C. and myself made small talk to keep Diego's mind off the ordeal ahead. Then the men came. Naked, he looked much older than his twenty-one years. Tall, lean, serious, his olive-skinned body was cocooned in heavy silk as two blue-chinned dressers, one in front and one behind, grasped the turquoise trousers and, lifting Diego off his feet, shook him into them as though they were sacking spuds. The silver embroidery sparkled like stars in the subdued light and as we looked, Diego appeared transformed, as though some new power was welling within him. Two *banderilleros,* one as corpulent as the other was tall, were smoking and talking about last week's fiasco in Alicante and next week's contract for a *pueblo* up north infamous, apparently, for its rain. J.C. gave his friend an affectionate hug as he went off to join his waiting *cuadrilla* in the big American car. We saw him again briefly, a solitary figure making his obeisance to the Madonna in the tiny chapel next to the emergency surgery, as we made our way to our seats in the shade of the president's box. Suddenly, all was a blaze of sight and sound as the multi-coloured parade of death entered the arena: and as always on these occasions, I couldn't get Lorca from my mind.

> * *A las cinco de la tarde.*
>   *Eran las cinco en punto de la tarde.*
> *Un niño trajo la blanca sabana*
>   *a las cinco de la tarde.*

"Candy is going to be late," Jesús said, looking anxiously at the empty seats to out left. "Diego must dedicate his first bull to him. He made it all possible."

How could I explain to someone who at times seemed more out of this world than in it, that every day the Candy entourage was getting through four or five times what it cost to set up Diego as a *novillero*? I didn't try. Instead, I concentrated on the first bull. The crowd were shouting their usual insults at the *picador*, as from his mounted height he tore at the animal's solid neck with his lance. But before my eyes was the image not of a lance, but of a syringe, as it pierced the far from solid Candy arm an hour before the show at the Casino, the big try-out before the up-coming tour of the U.S. of A. When it came to Diego's turn to face his first bull I saw him bow to the president, dedicate the kill to the absent Candy and then glance at the two empty seats to our left. There was no mistaking the disappointment on his face: but a moment later he was in the heat of battle. From the start, he displayed courage and natural style and when, seeing the inadequacy of the *banderilleros* with whom he had to work, he placed his own darts, the crowd loved him. And the cape work. Not once did the blue-chinned ones have to rush to his aid with flapping capes. He worked closer and closer to the animal, taking it through a breath-taking series of *veronicas* and *pase naturals*. The crowd was shouting for music. Above us, the president gave the nod, and the dance of death was transformed into a ballet whose ethereal beauty was frozen in the memory for all time. The thin, brassy sound of a *pasodoble* was drowned by the great roar that went up to the golden sun, '*Olé! O-lé! O--LÉ!!*' The dance stopped as abruptly as it had begun. Diego stood on the sand alone, except for that raging beast eight times his size.

> ** *Una espuerta de cal ya prevenide*
> *a las cinco de la tarde*
> *Lo demas era muerte y solo muerte*
> *a las cinco de la tarde.*

Only the cry of a solitary bird broke the silence as the youngster slowly raised his sword to eye level and began the line-up for the kill. Would he have the courage to stand his ground as the bull lunged at him head-on? Would the bull have the courage to attack the armed man? Man and beast remained motionless while, for what seemed like eternity, time stood still. When the climax came, it was all over in a matter of seconds. The gleaming sword made its mark, high up between the shoulder blades, and penetrated almost to the hilt. Moments later, his adversary sank in a pool of blood to lay dead at Diego's feet. The whole arena exploded in a rapturous ovation for the new star, and a sea of fluttering white handkerchiefs made their demand for a trophy, as the *banderilleros* escorted the youngster on a circuit of honour. But the only handkerchief I could see was the one held by Candy Floss in the wings at the Casino, as he spewed the vomit of fear before stepping into the battery of lasers to perform his act.

"Diego's got an ear! He's got an ear!" Jesús was yelling with excitement. "I wonder what's happened to Candy? He should have been here to see this . . . but what a party we'll have tonight!"

I prayed it would not be like the party I'd attended last night. The Villa Mimosa had been decked out for a *Well Hung Man* wake. There had been Candy's manager, Candy's agent, Candy's record label rep, Candy's publicist, Candy's music arranger, an assortment of session musicians, stage designers, lighting advisers, make-up artists, hair stylists, you name them and Candy had them, and had them, and had them. I remembered a woman with boobs so big she could balance a glass of fizz on them without spilling a drop, till Candy drove the scarlet rent-a-car into the nearest of the two pools, engulfing boobs and all in the tidal wave.

"They claim to collect anywhere," he said, looking at the sunken display of flashing lights. "And that's anywhere!"

An American with a crew-cut and double chin, clutching an iceberg of whisky, introduced himself as Candy's concert manager for the up-coming tour and pointed out the Candy personal secretary. "What buns that kid's got," he crooned. "He's just sitting on a gold mine and doesn't know it."

I wasn't sure about the last remark. Two drinks and a caviar canape later, the kid with the buns was using my tapes as carnival streamers. I went to rescue my day-in-the-life-of from the balcony whence they were being thrown. On the way, I passed a half open bedroom door. Inside was Candy, stripped off after his underwater drive and surrounded by what I assumed were rent-a-mechanics. The darkened room was filled with nervous laughter and the pungent odour of over-ripe bananas, as poppers popped, ampules crushed and hearts throbbed.

"Candy's definitely bisexual. He always has been and always will be," the Candy publicist said, taking my arm and leading me away.

"Sure," I said, "He likes men *and* boys!"

The trumpet sounding an *aviso* dragged me from my reverie. Diego was about to dedicate his second bull. I saw his look of dismay when he realized Candy was still absent. Then, for the first time since I'd met him, he smiled, and dedicated the bull to his friend, Jesús. I heard the scandalized whispers of the Málaga elite in the *sombre* seats around us, shocked that the dedicatee should be a mere stripling, and a *gitano* stripling at that.

"Show them, Diego! Show them!" Jesús cried, "Do it real good for both of us!"

I saw at once that Diego was going to have trouble. When placing the *banderillas* he had failed to correct the animal's tendency to lurch to the right with its twisted horn. Now, as he began to play it with his *muleta,* it passed more and more dangerously close to his lower abdomen as he defiantly held his body in a backward arch. Twice he nearly lost his balance as the vast beast lumbered by, leaving a trail of blood soaking into the turquoise suit of lights. Because the cape work was not executed with the same assurance as his first bull, the crowd turned sour. No longer were there shouts of *'Olé!'* and calls for *'Musica!'*. There was a smell of death in the air.

****¡Que no quiero verla!*
Dile a la luna que venga
que no quiero ver la sangre
de [Diego] sobra la arena.

The dark red stain was spreading down the youngster's upper thigh. *Send no Wreaths for a Well Hung Man*. My mind was filled with the image of the drugged and satiated Candy, his naked body being stimulated by mouths and hands to yet another climax, as the red wine of sacrifice was poured over his pallid flesh. Now the crowd was roaring that terrifying roar of massed humanity experiencing a vicarious gratification in the presence of death. I saw the twisted horn rise up with a fearful thrust, piercing Diego's slender body just beneath the ribs, lifting him in the air like a child's rag doll. And there he was, suspended, his life blood mixing with that of his adversary, as the *banderilleros* rushed forward waving their capes in a vain effort to distract the beast from its prey.

"Come back, you little fool!"

I had to physically restrain J.C. from leaping into the ring to help his friend. Instead, we raced down stone steps into the bowels of the ancient building, scattering tourists with their clean, sweet-smelling souvenir boxes of darts. In the stark, white infirmary a doctor was breaking an ampule. Over-ripe bananas. Would they stimulate Diego's damaged heart? Poppers could do nothing for the boy now. He lay there on the stretcher, soaked in blood, his olive skin an evil green in the blue light reflected by his beautiful clothes. He was, the doctor said, dead.

"No, no," Jesús said, "Sleeping. It's only a little sleep and he'll wake up soon."

The doctor's curt nod told me that I should take the youngster away: but J.C, stayed and, as I got a firm grasp on his arm, he leant over Diego and said in a calm, cool voice, "You're not dead. You're not dead! You're only sleeping!!"

"If you want to help Diego," I told him, "you will go and comfort his mother. Give her the ear Diego won when the crowd cheered."

On the way out, we passed the *matadero* where several sweating men were skinning and disembowelling the dead bulls. Suspended from a meat hook was a small radio. It was belting out Candy's latest hit. *'Send no wreaths. Yeah! Send no wreaths. Yeah! Yeah! For a well, well, well hung man.'*

I don't make a habit of encouraging young people to drink hard liquor, but I thought J.C. wouldn't get through the night without a large brandy. Somewhat to my surprise, he rejected it. He said good-night to me politely and went to his room, leaving me to settle down and work on the script for my next Radio Independiente Plus show. It was some time after midnight that I was rivetted by a voice on the radio.

"Here is a news flash. The novillero *pronounced dead by doctors after being gored at this afternoon's* corrida, *startled the night staff at the public mortuary by asking for a drink. He was*

---

* At five in the afternoon.
It was exactly five in the afternoon.
A boy brought the white sheet
at five in the afternoon.

** A basket of lime was already prepared
at five in the afternoon.
Everything else was death and only death
at five in the afternoon.

*** I can't bear to see it !
Tell night to fall.
I don't want to see the blood
of Ignacio in the sand.

– From *Llanto por Ignacio Sanchez Mejias*
by Federico Garcia Lorca.

immediately transferred to an intensive care unit at Carlos Haya."

As I hurried to J.C.'s room to wake him with the extraordinary news, he crashed into me on his way out.

"Where are you off to this time of night?" I demanded.

"Diego needs me," was all he said.

"He's been taken to Carlos Haya . . . ," but he didn't hear. He was already in the street. It was impossible for me to continue with my work, for one thing stuck in my mind: it was the intensity of the relationship between the two youngsters. How did J.C. know Diego was still in the land of the living? He didn't have a bedside radio in his room, telephone or any other kind of man-made communication. It was, in that pat phrase insurance companies so delight in using, an 'act of God'.

PAVO

I'D BEEN IN JEREZ to spend a couple of days with an old crony who'd been sent out from London by the advertising agency for which he wrote copy, to soak up the atmosphere of the annual Horse Fair. I'm pleased to say, it wasn't difficult to get him to soak up the atmosphere of the bodegas as well. As it happened, the weather was conducive to sipping a cool wine in the shade. The Spanish describe their climate as *'Ocho meses de invierno y quatro meses de infierno,'* (Eight months of winter and four months of hell). It was the first day of hell. All I wanted was for my pride-and-joy to shudder between my legs, let out a couple of loud farts, and die on me. It was my own damned fault. The alternator had been in need of attention for the best part of a month and I'd done f.a. about it. To make matters worse, I'd decided on the picturesque route back to Málaga, well clear of the *autopista*. So, here I was, kitted out in boot and denims, miles from that narrow strip of *costa* we know as civilisation, defenceless prey to the fierce heat of the afternoon sun. All around me were sloping hills of white *albariza* soil dotted with thousands of short, sturdy little Palomino vines. It was the time of year for the forming bunches of grapes to be sprayed; but no one was to be seen in the pulsing heat, as they took siesta after an alfresco meal under improvised canvas shade.

To the right, at the end of a narrow, pot-holed road, I could see a church tower. I began to push. The faded sign told me I was in Pavo. I continued pushing for a good five minutes before it struck me: Pavo is where J.C. was born! It was at the height of a particularly hot August. The family had to go to the provincial capital to get a *permiso* to operate a sawmill (in reality, one rusty blade driven by an equally rusty ex-Hispana-Suisse motor bike engine, but at the time Spanish bureaucracy was reeling under the iron fist of the *caudillo*). The *burro* was ailing and José's wife was with child. Had they a calendar, and had they been able to read, they would have known there was no chance of reaching Málaga and the comfort of the wife's relatives before J.C. came into the world. It was harvest time and the village was full of itinerant grape-pickers: and there was no room for them in the *posada*. Jesús was born in the fields under improvised canvas shade, such as I had just seen, and the juice of freshly crushed grapes was used as disinfectant by the attending picker-midwives. The boy child was wrapped in a picnic bread-cloth and placed in a grape basket, to be carolled with harvest songs played by the visiting Baza town band. Poor they may be, but who could ask for a more princely welcome into this world.

The poverty of the village told me it was just inside the Málaga province, for similar soil and similar grapes produce the dry, unfortified Montilla wine of neighbouring Cordoba, a wine protected by government quality controls, unlike Málaga, whose wine is unfashionably sweet. Few *extranjeros* living it up on the Costa know, or care, about the harshness of life only a jogger's stride inland. In spite of my sun-glasses, the white walls of the houses were almost blinding, while the sky above was a blue so deep it was almost black. Nothing stirred, not even a scavenging dog. Shutters and doors were tightly closed against the remorseless heat. Soaked in perspiration, I was desperate to find some shade.

"Hola! Hola!"

The voice, high pitched, almost girlish, floated from the top of the church tower, like a muezzin calling the faithful to prayer from his minaret. When I looked up, the owner of the voice had disappeared. A few moments later, a boy dressed in mechanic's overalls too large for him, a grease-stained Costa del Sol sun-hat perched on an unruly mop of auburn hair, appeared from the church doorway.

"Have you come from Torremolinos?" he asked breathlessly.

"Why do you think I've come from Torremolinos?" To say the least, the youngster's question had somewhat thrown me.

"I'm going to live in a great villa by the sea one day," he said with absolute conviction. "I'll swim all day and go disco dancing all night. I can see it all from up there . . . well, perhaps not *all* . . . but you can just see the sea."

My throat was crying out for a cold beer. I could have one in Torremolinos; but I knew that here, as in a thousand other Spanish *pueblos*, it would have to wait for the men to come back from the *campo* before there was anyone to open a bar. "Are you the mechanic?" I asked, certain there wouldn't be another.

"My dad is. But since he crushed his hand in the machinery at the co-op, I have to do all the work."

My heart sank at the prospect of this fledgeling getting stuck into my pride-and-joy, but I let him lead me to the small workshop behind the *panaderia*. At least it was cool inside. He scampered away and returned a few minutes later with a bottle of beer, so cold I almost dropped it.

"You're a mind reader," I told him. "What's your name?"

"Juan. But my friends call me Racha."

"Why Racha?"

"Because I'm like a gust of wind." He grinned. "But it's really short for *cucaracha* . . . because I get everywhere!"

When the father appeared, his hostility was immediately evident. He refused to even look at the machine, pretending he was only competent to fix the local mopeds; but Racha had already told me that, come September, they'd both be busy from dawn to dusk servicing the machinery, the tractors and the lorries that came to harvest the grapes.

"You'll have to arrange for a *portes* to come up from Málaga to collect it," the father said.

I was damned if I would! I stormed off in search of the Guardia Civil post which, as I suspected, was a small office attached to the living quarters for the *capitan*, his assistant, and their families. I presented my Radio Independiente Plus card and told him my problem. His problem was that the *dos amigos*, who know all there is to know about motor-bikes, were out of his area escorting the Tour of Spain race. But he sent his assistant to lean on the mechanic, and it was agreed the man would do the job if he could get the spares he needed from Antequera. A much travelled coach left every morning and returned every evening with mail, newspapers, parcels and exhausted shoppers. Like it or not, I'd have to stay in Pavo for a couple of nights at least.

"My dad doesn't like foreigners," Racha said, as he carried my recorder and overnight case to the hostel. "When I was smaller, I hid in a German caravan. I wanted to see the sea. But it was going in the wrong direction and the *dos amigos* had to bring me back."

I was not surprised to find that the hostel was run by Racha's mum and her widowed sister. It was an attractive old *posada* in an advanced state of dilapidation, with corridor after corridor of small rooms which, Racha assured me, were full every harvest time when the men came, which would account for why J.C. had to make his entrance in the harvest fields.

"I've given you the room next to mine," he said rather pointedly. "So we can talk. But not tonight."

"Why not tonight?"

"I have to keep Don Garcia company." I thought I saw his cheeks flush in the shadows. "He manages the bodega. His wife goes to Málaga every Thursday to be put on a kidney machine and doesn't return till Friday morning. Don Garcia is teaching me to play the guitar."

I heard the mother's voice from somewhere below calling *"Juan! Juan-ito! Juan-ITO!!"*

"Every time she thinks I'm making friends with someone, she finds something for me to do," he complained. "But aunt Tula's not so bad. I bet she bakes us some *magdalenas* before you leave!"

After I'd showered and put on a clean shirt, I went for a stroll round the village. The bougainvillaea-covered bodega; the church, with its corrugated plastic sheeting replacing long lost tiles; and the hostel, were the only buildings of importance. I had a drink in one of a score, or more, front-room bars, all of them offering the stark choice of the powerful local sweet wine or beer the strength of gnat's piss, and returned to the hostel to watch TV till the family meal was served at ten. The circular table was covered by a long, heavy cloth, beneath which my toes made contact with the brass Andalusian 'flame-thrower' which, come winter, would be filled with red-hot cinders to keep the diners' legs warm. We ate a goat's meat stew, pungent with wild herbs. The father ate noisily and said nothing, occasionally giving me little glances of open hostility. The mother didn't stop talking about the cost of everything since Spain had found democracy. And the aunt kept fishing for compliments for her culinary skill with the limited choice of ingredients. No one mentioned the absent Racha.

But as I left the table, the mother said, "I've moved your room to the other side of the building. Number fifteen. It's cooler and it's quieter. Juan had no right putting you where he did."

The following morning I tried to avoid the offered coffee, which I suspected had been stewed for several days in an aluminium saucepan and would be added to warmed-up goat's milk; but just as Racha had warned, Tia Tula had baked *magdalenas*. She anticipated my question by saying, "Juan will have his when he comes in from mass." She must have seen my raised eyebrows, for she added, "He blows the organ for Don Garcia and generally makes himself useful." My eyebrows remained raised.

"He seems to run this village," I said.

"We older folk can't read, or write, or add up," she went on, unashamedly including herself. "So he does the parcels for the post-bus every day, and since his big sister married a man from Jaen, I don't know how we'd run the hostel during the busy season without him. Then, not so long ago his father injured his hand. The workshop brings in the regular money. We couldn't afford hired help."

Fortunately, I had a first edition of Gide's *Corydon* I'd picked up in Jerez, albeit in French, so I decided to spend the morning in some shady spot reading. As I passed the church, I couldn't resist taking a look inside. The service was over, but there was the auburn-haired Racha in cassock and surplice, changing the altar candles. J.C. should see this, I thought. But before I could get to him to say good morning, I was intercepted by an old priest in a cassock green with age and flecked with snot.

"What a pleasure to welcome a stranger," he wheezed. "I fear ours is not a very interesting church, the village it too poor, you see."

"I didn't know the rich *could* enter the kingdom." Racha appeared to be masturbating a candle with a grease-stained hand, trying the whole time to attract my attention.

"They're all too wicked here to enter," the old priest went on, shaking his head sadly. "What few young people we still have, have been led astray. If Torremolinos is Sodom, then Pavo is surely Gomorrah."

I dropped a few coins in the offertory and made my escape, knocking into the confessional as I did so. What young sins had Racha told this harbinger of decay, I wondered? What innocent confession made him a prisoner of guilt? J.C.'s life had never been like this. I walked behind a row of white houses where women in black were vigorously sweeping their steps with besoms, and found a secluded place to read; but I'd barely read more than a couple of paragraphs before Racha found me.

"I have a letter from an English man," he said. "Will you tell me what it says? Please?" He'd changed into his mechanic's overalls and squatted with his thigh pressed hard against my thigh, as he held out the letter.

I knew it was an excuse to be with me the moment I saw the date. It was a good ten months old. From someone called Bert, in Swindon, offering to provide an air ticket if Racha could visit him for Yuletide snow and robins, fun and games, and fun, fun, fun. How was I to explain the Berts of this world to one so young? J.C. would instinctively find the right words; but he wasn't with me.

I was still struggling for suitable euphemisms when the mother's voice pervaded the entire village. *"Juan! Juan-ito! Juan-ITO!!"*

"I have to go," the boy said, "or she'll make dad's life hell for letting me out of the workshop."

Was it by accident, or divine intervention, that when I picked up the Gide, the book fell open at –

Do you think that St Augustine had a harder task to reach God because he gave his heart to a friend, who he loved as much as ever he loved a woman? Would you really claim that homosexual education of the children of antiquity exposed them to debauchery any more than heterosexual education does the school child of today? I believe a friend, even in the most Greek sense of the word, is a better influence for an adolescent than a mistress.

I didn't see Racha again till the dust-coated post-bus arrived from Antequera that evening. Somehow, the family contrived to keep him away from me. The spare parts needed to repair the alternator were exactly right, according to the father, and he promised to have the machine on the road again before midday the following morning. Sooner, with his xenophobia, I thought. In the hostel, the *comedor* was opened for the evening meal on account of two Telefonica engineers and a pesticide salesman having checked in for the night. Racha appeared from the kitchen precisely at ten carrying soup, thumbs held studiously erect, incongruously seductive in tight-fitting black trousers, scarlet sash and white silk bolero shirt. Who, I wondered, was he trying to seduce? I found out shortly after midnight, when I was woken by the sound of breaking glass. A foot had come through the closed half of my bedroom window. I shook myself awake and lurched towards the window, to be confronted by a pair of dangling legs in the same tight-fitting black trousers, but sans sash and sans bolero.

"You little idiot! Are you trying to kill yourself?"

Racha was hanging from the gutter, a guitar strapped over his shoulders, trying to get a foothold on the window-sill. I wrapped my arms around his slender waist and he slithered into safety.

"I had to come across the roof and there's not much of it left." he said. "But it doesn't matter. It will be ages before it rains again."

"Do you often go walking at night across the roof-tops?"

"They're always telling me I'm not to visit guests in their rooms. Won't I ever be old enough to know what I want?"

"What *do* you want, Racha?" I was beginning to panic. Half naked, old enough to be the boy's father, with the youngster's xenophobic father sleeping the sleep of the ignorant not many doors away: I knew damned well what Racha wanted, needed no doubt, even if he hadn't yet worked it out for himself.

"Record me for your radio programme and then I'll be famous and sing in the clubs along the Costa and have a villa in Torremolinos and swim in the sea and . . . "

"I can't record you *now!* The racket would be enough to waken the dead."

"I'll do it very, very quiet," he said. "I know how to do things . . . quiet. I don't have to go down and start getting the breakfast for another three hours at least."

"You're too young to know what you're talking about," I told him.

"Please!" he whispered in an unsteady voice and I noticed his right hand was unbuttoning his flies. "Please, *señor*, do something for me!"

I did. I seized the bedside water carafe and doused his fire. "I'm sorry to have to do that, Racha, but believe me, I'm not the one. Now get the hell out of here before you cause big trouble for both of us."

It was impossible to sleep after that. I lay awake aware that my rejection of the boy was little more than a private display of masochism. I was wallowing in some moral glow. I don't think Paul ever knew the truth about me in spite of our physical and emotional closeness over so many years. J.C. has come nearest to knowing me, in spite of my banishing thoughts of his sharing my bed. My *gitano* Jesús knows that love is fed by acceptance and not rejection: by this we become wiser than we know, better than we feel, nobler than we are. By which we can see life as a whole. By which, and by which alone, we can understand others.

The Harley roared to life again at exactly eleven thirty-five the following morning. Less than a mile down the

Málaga road I saw the *dos amigos* waiting in the shade of a fig tree, sitting at ease on their high-powered machines. They waved me down.

There was a creak of leather as the sergeant turned in the saddle to speak. "Everything done to your satisfaction, *amigo*?" he asked.

I sensed his companion eyeing me closely behind the anonymous darkness of his goggles. "She's performing as good as new," I said. "But the hostel charge was a bit steep."

"Let me see the bill."

As I took the piece of paper from my pocket and handed it to him, the companion's weather-beaten young face broke into a smile.

"But didn't Racha look after you?" the sergeant asked. "He looks after us. Very nicely."

"I'm not complaining," I said.

The glint of their steel handcuffs against the sombre olive green uniforms struck inexplicable terror in me, despite the brightness of the day. Suddenly, I knew the true meaning of freedom. As I turned a bend in the road, I saw the church tower in my driving mirror, rising above the brow of the hill. I could just make out the boy standing there, looking towards the sea, and thought I heard a cry of pain, like a muezzin calling the faithful to prayer, or a desperate soul in need of the freeing calm of a J.C..

The peasants of Pavo will tell you that, many years ago, one of their young men tried to run away from his obligations to family and to friends; but when they sent men with implements of steel to bring him back, the men were turned into pillars of chalk, which is why to this day their soil is so white and the fruit so impoverished. This they know to be true, because their forefathers told them so.

Si el mozo supiese . . . *

I'D LEFT PAVO in time to make Málaga for lunch; but as I was two days behind schedule already, and Mari-Carmen had delivered cold comfort when I'd called her the previous evening (assuring me that Tio Mac hadn't noticed my absence, thanks to the impressive stockpile of taped interviews I'd left with her) I decided to stop for lunch at one of my favourite *ventas* in the *montes*, not far from Antequera. As I was ordering a *manzanilla*, with a dish of olives for *tapa*, I remembered that the last time I'd been here it was with Paul. The thought depressed me. (Yes, Paul, I know, there's no going back.) I picked up a newspaper for company over the meal. It was two days old and I was about to put it down, when I saw two faces staring at me from the centre-fold that I knew all too well. One was the former *maletilla*, now headlined RISEN-FROM-THE-DEAD NOVILLERO, namely Diego. The other was my GIVER-OF-LIFE houseboy who, according to the lurid report, was now embarked upon a crusade to give back to the world (why not the whole universe while you're at it, J.C.?) all the good things it had given him. I looked again at the left-hand page. Diego recalled his hours in purgatory and hell: there were devils with horns, dilemmas aplenty, and a return to life in a Carlos Haya private ward – attended by a repentant and well-hung Candy Floss giving a private command performance of the new chart buster. With an olive stuck in my throat, I turned to the right-hand page. "We knew Diego wasn't dead but only sleeping," J.C. was reported as saying. "We urged them not to take him to the mortuary. This little body, balanced on a spinning world, 'tis but a glimpse of life we get which is immortal: and death,

---

* *Si el mozo supiese y el viejo pudiese, no habria cosa que no se hiciese.* (If the young man knew how and the old man was able, there would be nothing which wouldn't be done).

[Spanish proverb]

could we but seize on it like men, is life's greatest opportunity." What a load of old cod's wallop! And why the royal 'we'? Is the fledgeling daring to take on the mantle of the Holy Trinity?

"May I suggest that sir starts his meal with a little smoked *lucio* served with a soupcon of wild radish sauce?"

Good grief! They've installed a French *maitre-d*. Will the Spanish never learn that their country is *diferente*: and that makes it special? "I have an urgent date with a queer fish back in Málaga," I told him, giving the confused *patron* a soupcon of *duros* to cover aperitif and tip for his froggy import.

Hurrying to meet my queer fish, I had to swerve as I rode into the park to avoid a dog fight. A miniature Schnauzer was altercating with an Irish setter and a Great Dane, and somewhere in the middle of a tangle of leashes was J.C..

"I'm putting you in the dog-house for a start!" I shouted, coming out of a skid on a patch of tarmac that had melted in the heat of the day. When I'd showered and put on some clean clothes, I was not surprised to find he had already returned to the apartment and made a start on one of my favourite light meals – *huevos flamencos,* heavy on the *chorizo* and the yolks still runny. "When I left you in charge, it was with a list of things to be done. Not with a *carte blanche*!"

"I've done everything you wanted. Honest." He was very subdued, anxious to please.

"And how about the things I didn't want?"

Seeing him move about the apartment as he prepared and served my meal, I became increasingly aware of his almost mystical combination of strength and weakness. A frail body, but it was strong; deliberate, masculine movements, yet he moved with a feminine grace. It was quite the wrong time to be thinking such things, but as he served a blackberry flan which I knew he'd made himself, I wondered what sexual urges tormented him. He had made no attempt to seduce me since I rescued him from the machinations of the law, neither had he side-stepped any of those close contact moments of indecision that cannot be avoided when two people live together. I'd found it impossible to decide if there was, or was not, that electrifying *frisson* at moments when my naked flesh had inadvertently touched his. And it *was* inadvertent, for Jesús was somehow protected from the way of all flesh by his own timeless, highly polished, impenetrable silicon shell.

"You didn't want that report in the newspaper, did you, Mister Peter?"

"Did you want it?"

"Diego got us involved. He thought *corrida* spectators should be told something about death."

"And you believed that stuff about hell and grasping death by its bollocks? It was all true?"

His clear brown eyes didn't waver for a moment. "We don't say what we know to be untrue," he said. "But the reporter got it a little wrong."

"Like Matthew, Mark, Luke and John might have got it a little wrong?"

"We're all the children of our father and we make mistakes. Only our father is perfect."

"You were up Gibralfaro too long collecting berries. The height must have gone to your head." I tried to let him down as lightly as possible. "And another thing. If you can't control the dogs you walk, stop walking them. You know damned well I don't like dogs."

"You can give all you have for a pedigree pooch," Jesús said darkly. "But only love will make him wag his tail."

"Not so long ago we were conversing in proverbs, now apparently you're on a parable kick. Everyone has a right to his, or her, own belief. But please, leave me out of yours in future. Is that clear?"

"Yes, Mister Peter. Very clear."

At that moment, I knew I'd lost. I'd just hammered in the first nail.

I went into the studios to leave a pile of tapes I'd used in Jerez and Pavo for the back-room boys to ready for a final edit by Mari-Carmen. Transmissions had already reverted to the Spanish language for the evening, so I was surprised to find her still there.

"You owe me a drink," she said.

"You mean you want to talk," I said.

She deliberately steered clear of the usual RIP staff haunts. We had to gently nudge several women away from the entrance like cattle. Peasant modesty is still deep-rooted in Spain, even in the big cities. It would be a scandal for a decent women to enter a bar. She must wait for her man outside, no matter how long he tarries, unfed, unwatered and perhaps unloved. In front of the terraced houses on a hot summer night, no decent woman will sit outside on her favourite chair unless it is facing inward, for to look out on the passing parade would be brazen ungodliness. The men inside this spit-and-sawdust boozer were straining eyes and ears to know what we *jefe*-types were about. I was amazed my producer knew the place, let alone had the gall to lead a male *extranjero* there.

"Tio Mac's very unhappy with the spread in *Costa Tarde*," she said, watching the bubbles settle in wine freshly poured from the barrel rather than facing me, man to man.

"You don't think I'm *happy* about it, do you? If he had the editor fired, it would be no skin off my nose."

She made no attempt to drink the wine, but shifted her weight uncomfortably from one foot to the other. "As he's on the *Costa Tarde* board, he may well do that. The report didn't mention him; but it did mention you."

"And the old sod doesn't go for religious controversy?"

"It's not that, Pedro. It's the boy."

"What do you mean, 'it's the boy'?"

"Living with you."

"So?"

"Tio Mac is positively homophobic. I know the court decided you were a fit person to give him employment; but that's not the way Tio Mac sees it."

"Has he made you his bearer of ill-tidings?"

"Not exactly. He . . . suggested . . . I might point out the problem to you."

"It's his problem, not mine," I said.

She suddenly gulped her wine, as though she'd been on the wagon for months. "You're not alone," she said. "We all have to grin and bear his prejudices."

"You?"

"And Pippa. Surely you know we have a thing going for us."

"Yes. I thought the closet door was opened a month or two ago, but a gentleman doesn't mention such things to a lady."

"There's nothing gentle about you!" She made a little grimace. "But I think you're very courageous, taking on this *gitano*. Gay women have always been regarded as a bit of a joke. Besides, a woman can always be subjected to the legalized rape of marriage. But a gay man – if he chooses not to have children, that threatens the whole fabric of their society. You know better than I how shocked people like Tio Mac can be if two men show affection for each other in public. What you do on a park bench has to be much more discreet than what they do on the same park bench, often in the broad light of day."

I'd never expected Mari-Carmen to be so articulate. "You amaze me," I told her.

"I know Macasoli better than you. Don't forget I was his secretary. He'll believe it's his moral duty to sling mud. And he'll be praised by the priest in confession for doing so."

"The old sod's that religious, is he?"

"Grow up, Pedro! All bigots are!"

I offered her another drink, thinking maybe she wanted to blot out some of the miseries of the day, but she refused. We were just parting in the Lanes, when she ran back and jerked my arm. "I almost forgot to tell you. In spite of everything, he wants you to do a piece on a missing young American."

"Why me?"

"Because he thinks you Brits have a special relationship with the Yanks." She winked. "And he knows you have an eye for the boys."

I was woken the following morning by an insistent knocking on the apartment door. Not loud, but deliberate, the kind of knocking that was not going to stop till it received some attention. Where the hell was J.C.? The least he could do was to tell whoever was making the noise to desist, cut it out, fuck-off, or whatever was the most appropriate form of redress when he'd confronted the culprit. The little bastard would have to be reminded in no uncertain terms who was *jefe* around here. I looked at my watch as I struggled to put my nakedness into the royal-blue silk kimono Paul had brought back as a present for me when he'd worked for six months on some Panavision epic in Singapore.

"Are you aware it's not six yet! In the morning!" I bellowed before I'd even recognized the caller. And I might not have recognized him if it had not been for the wheel-chair, for Rafael looked more the young athlete in his chariot than the pathetic pile of lost youth I knew little more than a month ago. "Is that . . . .you . . . Rafael," I managed to get out.

"I'm terribly sorry to have woken you," he said. "I was calling for Jesús. We go swimming every morning."

My mind was blowing every kind of fuse as I tried to grasp reality. "You go swimming," I heard myself murmur.

"He's probably not back from Gibralfaro yet. He goes up there every morning. To meditate."

"You get your poor mum up at this hour to get you ready," I said, not that I felt all that well disposed towards her, or her sister, after the scene they made when J.C. first started the swimming lessons.

"They're both still asleep," he said. I must have been looking like some sort of goon, because he added anxiously, "I can wash and dress myself now."

"That's good," I said, and the moment I'd said it realized how inadequate 'good' was to describe something little short of a miracle. "That's great, wonderful, wonderfully great." Words just gushed from me, all of them totally out of control.

"I have Jesús to thank for that. He *made* me do it. My mum and my aunt mean well, but they've never *made* me do anything."

I was getting my thought processes geared up for the day now. "What does your doctor say about it?" I asked.

My next question would be what did Rafael's mum say about it, for the thick lady was rapidly losing the cross she had had to carry for the past twenty-something years; and from what I knew of women, and this woman in particular, she would not willingly give up her noble suffering. It was the only thing society admired her for, her suffering.

"The doctor says some times these things happen, and you get back the use of parts of you that have never functioned before," Rafael was saying. "He didn't know why. But he knew it couldn't be Jesús."

"What do you think?"

"Everything works when Jesús is around. He does nothing for me, unlike my mum, who does it all. But it works . . . he knows *how*. "

I was about to pop the question of what his mum thought about Jesús, when the *gitano* miracle-worker himself returned from his meditation. "I'll breakfast out this morning," I told him. "Your pupil is here for his swimming lesson and an early start might make it easier for me to find a lost heir. That's the H-E-I-R variety for those still learning the lingo." I could see the two youngsters hadn't a clue what I was talking about. "Neither is it the kind that is jugged, nor the species that turns prematurely grey."

J.C.'s face broke into a mischievous smile. "Who's turning prematurely gay?" he asked.

There was no doubt that daddy Oliver was going to stir things up over his missing heir. The big American, boss of Consolidated Latex, had flown in from Detroit with his curvaceous wife and angular future daughter-in-law, checked in at the national *parador* with its superb view from Gibralfaro across the bay to Torremolinos and beyond, and proceeded to demand instant action from everyone to locate Gregory Hervey Oliver Junior. Greg was twenty-three, had left Yale as far as I could tell with more muscle than sense, and had been doing Europe for six months before settling down to marriage and getting stuck into daddy Oliver's latex.

"We booked a transatlantic call person-to-person for his

birthday," Mrs Oliver wailed, "But the hotel denied ever seeing him. Yet he wrote to us only ten days ago on the hotel's own note-paper."

"And the damned reception clerk accused my son of having stolen it, like some common hippy," Mr Oliver boomed. "I'll have his hide!"

I glanced at the love-you-all-everything's-fine note. I knew the hotel well. The Pabellon was an old place off the Torremolinos central *plaza,* up market in its pricing but definitely down market in the cosmopolitan set it attracted to its disco, formerly an English style tea room. In short, the Pabellon has 110 of the 152,582 hotel beds currently on offer on the Costa, from Almeria in the east to Estepona in the west.

"It's inconceivable that Greg couldn't look after himself," the bride-to-be chipped in. "He was a judo green belt."

Her name was Nestor. I gathered her father made things with daddy Oliver's latex, doubtless prophylactics, but I didn't ask. "What was his scene when he wasn't on the mat?"

"He's crazy about disco dancing and he's a super scuba diver." She obviously hero-worshipped him. I decided I could hero-worship him too, when she gave me the photographs of the hunky young man in his judo robe and scuba diving gear.

"Do you know where he's been before Spain?" I asked.

"We had postcards from London, Paris France, Hamburg, Rome and, just before we left the States, two from Marrakech," Mrs Oliver told me.

I promised to mention their missing son next time I was on air, in the hope that one of my listeners may know his present whereabouts. I left them trying to make an appointment with the top man in the Guardia Civil, though I could have told them that policemen the world over do little about missing twenty-three-year-old sons with a green belt till they are presented with some genuine cause for concern.

Within twenty minutes of my reference on air to the missing heir, I was being summoned into the presence of Tio

Mac himself. I'd often seen the boss of Radio Independiente Plus arrive, and depart, through automatic glass doors that had a knack of expressing their own opinion of the round blob of a man by (on average six times out of ten) managing to sandwich him between them; but communications between us had so far been left to the not always linguistically adept Mari-Carmen. He was smoothing down an alpaca jacket after yet another altercation with the doors as I entered, expecting a dressing down for my execrable pun on h-air. Instead, I was accused of having staged a kidnapping. To say the least, I was speechless. Momentarily.

"This person has phoned the station and said you have the American boy hidden away in some shack up Gibralfaro." Señor Don Alvarez José Macasoli drew himself up to his full height, which wasn't much, and stormed.

"And what am I supposed to be doing with him?"

"You're getting us bad publicity."

"There's no such thing as *bad* publicity! You should know that. Sir." I added the 'sir' in the hope of placating him, but he went storming on.

"*Gitano* boys is bad publicity."

"I've given employment to *one* boy. What we may, or may not, do together . . . "

"I don't give a damn what you do together, so long as you don't frighten the dogs," Tio Mac wheezed.

"You mean horses. It's a well known quote."

"I know what I mean!"

"The other well known quote you might find useful some time is the college after-dinner speaker, in the presence of royalty, referring to 'our queer dean'."

"I won't have you ruining our business! Are you, or are you not, a practising homosexual?"

"No, I'm very experienced, thank you." And with that, I walked out on him.

As I didn't know if I was still in a job, or out of one, and didn't much care one way or the other, I returned to the apartment, intending to have a shower and indulge in a pleasure I'd had little time for in recent months – listening to some treasured old LPs of Flagstad *et al.* doing battle against the mythical Tio Macs of this world. But it was not to be. A rag-bag of dripping wet humanity was jammed in the doorway and spilling over the pavement into the road. In the middle of it all was J.C., arms waving like a windmill, head so vigorously shaking in the negative mode I feared it would fall off at any moment, but quite definitely dry.

"What the devil's happened?" I asked, pushing a squelchy fat woman and an eel-like man to one side.

"They followed me," Jesús said. "I can't make them go away. They just keep coming."

"Go to your own homes! This is private property!" I shouted hopelessly. Not surprisingly, the crowd jostled J.C. even more. The fat woman and the eel man were looking at me resentfully.

"He saved my daughter's life!" a woman's voice cried out.

"He walked on the water to reach her!" came a more distant cry: and, "He's a shining example of today's youth, he is."

But there was also the voice of dissent. "Fraud!" "He used a surfboard!" "Where do you hide your water-wings, matey?" Someone threw what looked like an over-dead fish.

"What are they on about, J.C.?" I demanded. "I want to know exactly what you've been up to."

"It's nothing to worry about, Mister Peter," Jesús said, recovering much of his sang-froid. "I was walking along the harbour wall, when I saw a little child fall off one of the mooring buoys in the outer harbour. We reached out for her and lifted her to safety."

"He walked on the water to do it!" a voice said again: and another, "He's a blooming magician!"

"Who's 'we', J.C.? Who was with you?"

"Me and our father," was his simple reply.

Just then, a kid with glasses and a notebook pushed in and asked, "It's been suggested you used a surfboard to reach her. Is that true, or false?"

"Don't answer that, J.C.," I said.

"He's our friend from the *Costa Tarde,*" Jesús explained.

"He's no friend of mine!" I yelled, and turning to the bespectacled one asked, "Are you Matthew, Mark, Luke or John?"

"Fernando, *señor,* " the kid replied.

"Get inside and lock the door, and don't come out till I tell you to come out," I told J.C..

He did his best to obey me, but two women and a photographer were blocking the front door and the wet mob on the steps were making it difficult to move in any direction. A Spanish youth next to me had a T-vest with the English slogan: WINDSURFERS DO IT STANDING. I'd heard of scuba divers doing it deeper, students doing it by degrees, even hang-gliders doing it higher . . . what a time to get involved with a hot-blooded windsurfer, who was making it very clear by the way he was pressing the hard-on in his shorts against my thigh, that he'd do it any way to get his rocks off.

"He's an angel from God," a woman said, crossing her ample bosom as she said it.

"Get inside!" I urged J.C. again. The flashes from the camera were like the deity's lightening going through me. I felt the hot wet semen of the boy pressing against me soak my thigh, as some distance away a taxi drew up, Mari-Carmen got out and began battling her way towards us, wielding a clipboard.

"The relief of Mafeking . . . am I glad to see you!" I said.

"I heard about your row with Tio Mac," she said, gasping for breath. "We have a lot of different listener reactions. So I grabbed a cab and brought them for you to see." She looked angrily at the representative of *Costa Tarde,* who appeared to be picking his nose. "Who's he?" she demanded.

"He, I believe, is the good time that was had by all!"

God bless the inventor of sleep, the cloak that covers all men's thoughts, the food that cures all hunger . . . the Knight again! . . . the balancing weight that levels the shepherd with the king and the simple with the wise. I don't know who among us was the simple and who the wise, but I do know that if, having struggled to get Jesús into the safety of the apartment, Mari-Carmen had not discreetly left us, if not to sleep, to cat-nap our way back to the equilibrium, I for one and I suspect J.C. for two, would have blown a fuse. As it was, I felt the electricity of life pulsing through my body, as my head cleared and I realized J.C. was laying in my arms, we both on the black leather couch, my rough-skinned face brushing the bloom of his warm cheek. I pulled away, in an awakening panic that I might act towards him in a way I had told myself I never would. As I did so, I felt his lips move and press against the lobe of my right ear, as his hands tried to stop my breaking the embrace.

As I got to my feet, he asked, "Why are you afraid of me, Mister Peter? Is it because of Paul?"

I felt a chill run down the sweat in the small of my back. "You're too young to understand," I said, fearful that this strange youth understood all too much.

"If we don't love each other, who we see every day, how can we love our maker, who some of us may never see?"

"There is more than one kind of love," I said evasively.

"There is only one." The way he said it struck terror in me. All I could think of was the patchwork bed-cover his mother had given us at our *juerga* in this very room. It was for a double bed.

"I can't debate ethics with you now," I said. "You can see for yourself the pile of stuff my producer has left for me to go through."

I picked up the clipboard Mari-Carmen had put on top of the word processor and started to read the summary of listener calls about the missing Yank. One of them flashed at me like a neon sign: "The secretary of Jah remembers him." Who, or what, was Jah? The Spanish go berserk on their acronyms. I was about to try to get Mari-Carmen on the blower when J.C. coolly informed me it was a snob judo club – Judo Aficionados Hispanico – out at Benalmadena. He knew it, because a cousin used to work there as a towel-boy. I hadn't time to wait to hear the intriguing end of the story, I was on the Harley heading in the scorching afternoon sunshine for the club. The secretary was like so many club secretaries in Spain, a retired policeman or civil servant, trustworthy, efficient, but totally lacking enthusiasm for, or knowledge of, his members activities. We sat in his air-conditioned office and he insisted on waiting for a glass of chilled *fino* and a dish of anchovy-stuffed olives to be served, before indulging himself in the pleasure of being of assistance to someone as important as a representative of Radio Independiente Plus. How was Señor Don Alvarez José Macasoli,who did so much to promote Spain, and Andalusia in particular? I wanted to say he was in a firing mood today: instead, I muttered something about sending his regards and hoped the old fool wouldn't spot my pride-and-joy parked under the fig tree at the top of the drive. It was next to a no-parking sign that I'd swear in a court of law (and I'd probably have to if the secretary knew Tio Mac as well as he pretended he did) wasn't there when I arrived.

"We organised the first Costa del Sol judo championships last month," he was saying. "We had entries from all over the world. Even a Japanese policeman. And our own Foreign Legion entered a team. It was highly successful, highly successful."

He chewed contemplatively on an olive.

"And this American boy?" I prompted.

"I have his entrance papers here." He opened a folder and passed them to me. "He was very good. Beat the Legion's champion. But not the kind of person we like to see in the sport."

"Why do you say that?"

"He's a *sodomita*," he said.

"How do you know?"

He preened his hair-line moustache. "I pride myself in recognizing a pervert as soon as I see one. Besides, he made an ostentatious display of entertaining the legionnaire in the club restaurant. I had to authorize his credit card for the best part of twenty thousand pesetas."

Nothing irritates a certain class of Spaniard more than the sight of a foreigner in his country with 'funny-money' to burn at the end of the month when, traditionally, the

Spanish themselves have to tighten their belts till next pay day. As I write, the Torremolinos road-sweepers have come out on strike because the town hall is two months behind in paying them their monthly dues. At the other end of the human scale of values, I know a man who has five thousand horses which he can lend to a film unit at a moment's notice, but try to borrow a fiver from him . . . he hasn't the cash, he'd have to borrow it first from a friendly road-sweeper. Early in the month.

I thanked the obnoxious Jah secretary for the photocopies of the contest papers and left before he had time to recognize another *sodomita*. I rode up the winding mountain road to Ronda where, in 1493, the Maestranza, a corporation of knights, established bull-fighting as an art. Now a new corporation swaggers down the narrow streets in grey-green uniforms, shirts open to the belly-button, displaying macho chests; and red tassels dangling from forage-caps, forcing every head to stay erect. For Ronda is the HQ of Spain's North African elite, and I had to find just one man, a judo champion named Felix Espelosin.

Vultures were hovering over the Tajo gorge as I swung into my first bar. "I'll roll you on the mat for a thousand pesetas, *amigo.* " There was a lot of good-natured laughter at the expense of what they thought was a foreign quean looking for trade; but two of them took me seriously and agreed to take me to a bar where the guys who enjoy punishing their bodies hang out. I bought several more rounds of the semi-sweet brown Pedro Ximenez wine and tried blotting it up with the *chorizo tapas*, or I'd never get back to Málaga safely on two wheels. Eight bars and eight drinks later, I found my cat.

"I know an American friend of yours, Felix," I told him, hoping I wasn't pushing the truth beyond credulity.

"You want me to give you a work-out?" He was a good six-foot-three, broad shouldered, with a deep scar over his right eye. "How is Greg? He didn't leave any message when he checked out of the Pabellon."

"Let's walk," I said. I didn't want to rake dirt in public.

We walked in the setting sun along the rock path above

the gorge, and I admitted I'd never met Greg. "The hotel denies he ever stayed there."

"But that's crazy! We went to his room together –" The pock-marked face, deeply tanned by the outdoor life, broke into a boyish grin.

"And screwed?"

Relieved that I understood these things, he said: "Hell, we fucked! Near busted the bed!"

"Good for you. But it cost him more than he expected."

The legionnaire's face lost the boyish grin and the scar over the eye appeared to flicker like a red warning light. "Don't get me wrong, mate. I didn't encourage him to spend all that on expensive wine and food. To be honest, I can't tell the difference between a *brik* of Jumilla and a fancy import from France."

"I can." I was beginning to like the young man. "I prefer the Jumilla."

Far down in the gorge the dark shadows obscured the matchbox houses from view, while the reddening sun up where we were walking was turning the green of the soldier's uniform a dark purple. He had stopped to urinate. There was no one else about and he deliberately stood giving me a full view, letting the whole organ swing free of his flies. He shook the last drops free using his left hand, as would an Arab, and then began to give it a few stimulating strokes.

"I'm hung like a horse," he said. "You want a session now?"

"I've something more important in mind," I told him. "I want you to check in with me at the Pabellon tomorrow night."

"Few things I enjoy more than a large bed . . . and a guy in it, waiting for me."

"You're missing the point, *amigo,*" I said, irritated by his unnecessary exhibitionism. "We're going to find out why the hotel denies that Greg ever stayed there."

"I can't get a pass, just like that."

"You've got a grannie, haven't you?"

"She's dead."

"Then let her die again."

His eyes were wild, like a trapped animal. I had a momentary vision of my body being hurled into the gorge, for he was still on heat. I could see it throbbing behind the coarse cloth of his trousers with a life of its own. I was switched on with the adrenaline of fear and lust combined, and desperately wanted to yield to whatever sexual aggression he had in mind.

"I daren't get involved with *extranjeros*," he said. "It could ruin my career."

"You'll get involved with me!" Guys like this who have their fun, but offer nothing in return, really make me see red. "Understand this, Felix. I'll personally do for one of your nine lives, if I don't see you tomorrow in Torremolinos."

Not surprisingly, Felix stopped purring and lost his erection.

The ride back to Málaga was foolhardy in the dark, on two wheels. The mountain road is old, twisted, narrow and accommodates more than its fair share of road hogs, who delight in weaving an unsteady path from disco to disco, taking the longest route and attempting to negotiate it in the shortest time. It's their choice, if they wish to depart this world via the Ronda gorge; but they won't take me with them. I had a steady ride, thinking of a hot shower ahead and placing odds against myself in the matter of Felix-the-cat and his Yankee sex-mate. I was far from certain he'd show, and if he didn't, my chances of proving the Pabellon at fault in some way were slender indeed. It wasn't till I'd come out of the shower that I saw dead Paul looking at me across the bedroom. Someone had put his photo on my bedside table. That someone could only be J.C..

"How dare you do a thing like that!" I bellowed, when I'd dragged him from the kitchen where he was preparing the evening meal. It wasn't so much the photograph but a ghost I'd seen, that outward manifestation of an inward fear.

"I found it in a drawer when I was putting your laundry away," he said. "You still need his love. You rejected mine."

I was about to say "You don't know the first thing about

love" but stopped myself in time; it would have been deliberately cruel, and J.C. had already disturbed my emotions in a way they had never been disturbed before. It wasn't his fault that the only lifeline youth can throw out is spun of good intentions. If the young man knew how . . .

"I feel too tired to discuss it tonight," I said. "Put the photograph back where you found it, please, and we'll forget it."

"You can never forget a memory, Mister Peter. Memory, like life itself, is part of eternity."

"Uncle Tom Cobbleigh and all, are part of eternity. I don't know where you get all this crap from J.C., but if you're not careful it'll send you bonkers."

I did what I invariably did when Paul was alive and I wanted to avoid an argument – I turned the radio on to the BBC World Service and pretended to be interested in the latest report from Wogo-Wogo-land. We ate in silence, except for the scraping of cutlery on the plates, the over-cultured voice of the news reader and the rumbling of J.C.'s tum as he gulped mouthful after mouthful in some childish race to be first to be finished and, so, first to bed. We both knew I had lost before the race had even begun because, whereas J.C. could look me steadily in the eyes without betraying a blemish within, I could not similarly return the purity and innocence of his gaze. Age has too much to hide. When you're a kitten, I told myself, you can piddle on the carpet: when you're a cat, you can't.

It was a dreadful night. I fell into a restless sleep sucking indigestion tablets and woke about three. The all-night bars had not yet emptied and the city was quiet. So quiet that I could hear a soft cry of pain: at first, out of focus, as though it was an injured animal in the park; and then closer, like a lonely puppy-dog asking to be let in. I lay in the darkness for several minutes. The cries and whimpers went right through me, so that I began to share the pain. There was no doubt, now that the agony was in focus, that it was coming from J.C.'s room. I got out of bed and walked bare-footed over the cool tiles to the little room that used to be the workshop for my pride-and-joy before J.C.

moved in. The cries were quicker, staccato, with gasping intakes of breath. As I opened the door, I saw he was laying on top of the sheets, naked, the moonlight pouring through the open window to splash over and bejewel his slender brown body. The swollen cock was pulsing with a life of its own on a cushion of curly black hair. As I approached him, I saw the twisted lines of pain in his face. The agony he was suffering made him appear to be an old man. I looked again at his beautiful manhood. The trails of semen, copious in its discharge, made clear what he had been doing. I gently took hold of the organ and the tightness of the foreskin at once betrayed the cause of pain. The poor kid was suffering from phimosis, so that every ejaculation brought pain instead of pleasure.

He was fully awake now. "Please, no," he gasped, pushing my hand away from his cock.

"Why haven't you told someone about this, you little fool?"

"It's how our father made me, Mister Peter."

"Then it was a botched job." I picked up the edge of the bed-sheet and began mopping up the glutinous fluid. "You don't have to suffer like this. One little nip of the doctor's knife and a few days parceled up like an Egyptian mummy, and you'll have a piece of equipment of which to be proud."

"But doesn't it cost a lot of money to . . ."

"Stop jabbering! After breakfast, we're going to get you to the nearest clinic and find a sympathetic doc. who'll treat it as a thing of beauty, which it is, and have it working properly without depriving you of that jewel-box called a foreskin."

Which was how I started my day, taking J.C. like a horse to be shod, to a new medical centre in Fuengirola. I never cease to be amazed at the number of Spaniards who suffer phimosis because of the embarrassment, the cost of surgery, the fear of any doctor, all because the Christian, unlike the Arab or the Jew , is not compelled by his religion to be circumcised. Apart from the denial of pleasure involved, it can cause enough psychological hang-ups, to say nothing of matrimonial problems, to provide several thousand psychologists with a life-time's devoted work.

I looked at the day's papers while I waited for J.C. to have the mechanics of his manhood put right. Several of them had picked up the missing-young-American story, featuring a variety of pictures of the distraught fiancée. Would she ever know she had a wayward husband, I wondered? Doubtless if, or when, Greg turned up she would have a husband, for wealthy American families could be very persuasive. I took J.C. out for a celebratory lunch and persuaded him to cut down on the coke for fear he would be constantly waking his Egyptian mummy. Then I went over to Torremolinos early to make sure of a room at the Pabellon, for the season was beginning to pick up and like all the other hostelries on the Costa, the Pabellon was sure to have double-booked. It didn't take long for me to discover that the management wanted to be all things to all people: an efficient reception guarded the ground floor elevators, but by walking up to the mezzanine American Bar and cafeteria, anyone could gain entrance to the second floor elevators. And anyone did, from ladies of the night plying a little *merienda* trade, to acne blighted students engaged in some extra curriculum activities.

"Do you remember Greg's room number?" I asked Felix when he joined me shortly after eight. A couple of German queans were licking their lips at the bar, envious of my apparent good fortune.

"Sorry, no. But it was the fourth floor."

"You remember the door, don't you?" He was as stupid as he was handsome.

The whole of the fourth floor appeared to be abandoned. There were no flowers on the landing and no chamber maid in the service room. But Felix seemed sure of the door, yes, it was Room 22, he was quite sure about that now because he recalled thinking that would be his age next birthday. I took him to my room on the fifth and called room service for a couple of *Cuba libres*. I hoped maybe he'd recognize the waiter, or the waiter recognize him, but no dice. So I rang for the chamber maid. She was an elderly woman who'd seen it all and didn't think much of any of it, in no mood to disobey an instruction that no guests were allowed on the fourth floor, till a thousand peseta bank-note reminded her that some things were still worth seeing. I didn't know what I was going to find in Room 22. What I had not expected was there would be nothing to find. The room was completely empty. Curtains, carpet, furniture, everything had gone: and walls, floor, ceiling were clinically white, like one was standing in a boundless cube. I had a sudden vision of blood splattered on the whiteness and quickly closed the door. I returned to my room on the floor above to find Felix naked, except for an athletic jock and a small gold crucifix hanging round his neck.

"What the hell do you think you're doing?" I asked.

"I haven't had it off for a whole week," he said, striking a pose and caressing his jock pouch with his left hand.

"You're here for one damned reason alone! To help me find Greg!" The Spanish may be good Catholics: but if they were all like this one, I thought, the confessionals must overflow. "For crissake get your clothes on, we're about to attack!"

I shall long cherish the memory of the look on the young reception clerk's face when I told him that the legionnaire who accompanied me had fucked Gregory Hervey Oliver Junior in Room 22 of his hotel and we wanted to see the director. The director did his best to pull rank, accusing Radio Independiente Plus and my programme in particular, of stirring up a hornets' nest when no hornets' nest needed to be stirred. He would be in touch with my *jefe* and doubtless my *jefe* would be in touch with me, and please to leave his hotel as he didn't want legionnaires or anyone else giving it a bad reputation, and please to cease trying to corrupt his reception staff which was known throughout the whole of Torremolinos to be incorruptible. And with that, I was shown the door.

I told Felix he could keep the room till midday and left him some loose change for tips; whether, or not, he corrupted the reception staff I didn't much care, but I was certain the youngster would spend the rest of the evening cruising. I didn't know it then, but the rest of my evening was to be spent in a police station. I sensed trouble as I locked up the Harley outside the apartment. There were no lights on and the radio wasn't blaring out *flamenco*, both of which would have been in order had J.C. been at home, as he most certainly should have been. I was sorting out my keys when a bundle of flowing robes lurched towards me from the entrance hall. I thought at first it was Mari-Carmen in one of her more bizarre evening toilets, but then I recognized Dolores le Grande, J.C.'s mum, and remembered she was to sing *saetas* in the cathedral this evening, part of an international seminar on Folk Song and Religion organised by the University of Málaga. I'd promised to turn up, but it had completely escaped my mind, and with the events of the past twenty-four hours, I suspected it had escaped J.C.'s mind as well. But it wasn't our absence she was on about: it was J.C.'s far from wanted presence.

"They've taken him to the *comisaria*! " she gasped. Then, getting nothing but a stunned silence from me, grabbed me by both arms and shook me. "Don't you understand? They've arrested my Jesús!"

"Who have? Why? What happened?"

"He came to the cathedral to hear me sing and they wanted to charge him a thousand pesetas. He knew I wasn't getting a performance fee, one doesn't on these occasions, not in front of the Virgin, but they have to meet their expenses."

"And I hadn't left him sufficient money?"

"No, no it wasn't anything like that. He refused to pay and made a terrible scene. Shouted something about turning our father's house into a *feria caseta*. And then went on to accuse the church hierarchy of all kinds of things, from using imported luxury cars for their vanity, to purchasing rare sacramental wines for their gluttony. He made a terrible, terrible scandal. It took six cathedral officials to restrain him. And then the *policia* arrived and took my Jesús away. I think it's all my fault. I should never have agreed to the engagement in the first place. What shall I do? What *can* I do now?"

"If it's anyone's fault, it's mine," I told her. "He was

circumcised today. I shouldn't have left him alone."

She was looking twenty years older than when I last saw her, possibly because she had not put on cosmetics for her cathedral appearance. "What will happen to him now? Will he have to go back to jail?"

"I hope not," I said. "You try to get some sleep. I'll get cracking on the legal niceties, if anything is nice about this whole ghastly mess."

Which was how old Don Luis came to be called for a reprise of his legal eagle performance at the witching hour of three in the morning. He was, indeed, a magician, instinctively picking the right officials to drag out of bed, the right words to use, and the right promises to be made.

"They won't want to spend a day, or more, writing reports, only to charge him with acts that many people wish they had the courage to perform themselves," Don Luis said.

And he was right. Come the dawn, they gave him a metaphorical kick up the backside and handed him back to me for safe keeping.

"Aren't you ashamed at the way you upset your poor mother?" I asked him, as we left the *comisaria* together.

"I was right, Mister Peter," was all he would say. "You know I was right."

As the director of the Pabellon had predicted, my *jefe* was in touch with me – at the unusual hour (for my *jefe*) of eight, in the morning. Tio Mac was fussing like an old hen when I presented myself in his office. "There's no need to panic," he clucked. "Everyone must keep calm. That's it, there'll be no trouble for anyone if we all keep calm."

Mari-Carmen sat lovingly at the side of the desk and put on her best being-calm act. It was, Tio Mac began, unfortunate that first reports had implicated me in the American boy's disappearance; but it had been a catastrophe for the hotel when Gregory Harvey Oliver Junior had arrived from Morocco incubating cholera.

"We've had four years of drought," Mari-Carmen chipped in. "The public health authorities have been expecting something like this to happen. And dreading it."

She was doing her best to gain my sympathy. "You know better than anyone, Pedro, how the British newspapers would relish such a story."

"It would cripple the economy," Tio Mac went on. "The hotels would lose millions of pesetas and thousands of people would be made unemployed. But the director of the Pabellon has covered up for everyone. Brilliantly."

"Dazzling," I said. "And how about the medical profession in all this? How much did their brilliant performance cost?"

Tio Mac warmed to his revelations. The doctor had covered up (for a consideration) by removing his patient to the convent of the Holy Sisters of the Bleeding Heart in the *montes* near Coin, and the Holy Sisters had covered up (for a consideration) by not reporting the potential danger to public health to the appropriate authority. The appropriate authority had covered up for the tourist board which had covered up for the *ayuntamiento* which had covered up for . . .

"How's the patient?" I cut in.

He was, Tio Mac assured me at his most pontifical, making a good recovery and could be flown back to the States in a few days time. "But you can't use any of this on the air," he added.

"You mean I'm being muzzled?"

"Nice people don't want to hear about nasty diseases and sexual aberrations."

"For a consideration?"

He smiled sympathetically. Nothing is worse than Tio Mac's sympathetic smile. "The hotel chain's booking peak time, yes."

"And I'm the consideration!"

Perhaps it was my silence over lunch that told J.C. something was wrong. "Every man's the son of his own deeds," he said. "And since I am a man, I can become pope."

It might have been Paul quoting the Knight of the Sad Countenance. It was supposed to cheer me up. It didn't.

BLOOD WEDDING

THE BROWN-FACED silver whiskers had lost his whiskers for the special occasion: one of his thirty-two great grandchildren had shaved him, protesting volubly, with the blade they used on the skin of wild boar after the hunt, after the kill. He had stood, clinging to the altar rail, throughout the entire ceremony in the little baroque church between the pine trees and the *autopista,* in the foothills of the *montes,* less than an hour's drive from the city centre. His twinkling blue eyes missed nothing of the strange religious ceremony the Heredias clan had insisted should be performed, if one of theirs was to be joined to one of his. His withered, parchment-like ears picked up considerably less of the mumbo-jumbo. 'With this ring I do thee wed' was just about acceptable, though didn't some African tribes pierce the noses of their women to wed them? What shattered his ninety-four years of life experience was the ceremony of the bread and wine. 'This is my body . . . this is my blood . . . '

"They're cannibals!" silver whiskers declared, as one of his great grandsons handed him his head man's *bastón,* and helped him into position to lead the Rivas clan into the fresh air beyond these four confining walls.

Outside the tiny church were a few scattered wooden houses, too old for memory to know why they were built and who built them. There was no road, merely a track that led deeper into the pine forest. There were no shops, or bar, or telephone, unless one walked over rough land to the *autopista;* but there was a kind of storehouse, windowless, built of corrugated iron sheets, a kaleidoscope of paint betraying its casual use, the concrete dance floor as hard to the foot as it was unsympathetic to the eye. This parking lot for no-man's-land was used once a year, in late December, for the unique peasant song contest known as the Fiesta de los Verdiales. Now it was the scene of a much publicized *gitano* cementing together of two dynasties, recorded for posterity in the headline of one British tabloid – RIVAS OF BLOOD WEDDING. For Bruno Rivas, still known to his family and intimates by his first name, Honorio, was the Bruno Rivas whose weekly TV and radio *flamenco* show is syndicated worldwide making enough for its sponsors to buy out a major Hollywood film studio and, for Honorio, a Mexican-style *hacienda* hidden among the white villages north of Cadiz. J.C. was there because he was an Heredias. I was there because I was J.C.'s friend. Mari-Carmen was there because she had swiped the RIP accreditation. Pippa was there because Mari-Carmen couldn't do justice to anybody's anything without an assistant. And Douggie Hardman was there with a party of British and American wine writers, plus several crates of his export plonk.

Carla del Montes, the mother of the bride, began the *copla* she had composed for the occasion. In the dark under the stars, the wedding guests took up the rhythm, clapping it out, doubling and redoubling the beat. It is said that man is born with natural music – the beat of his heart – but has to learn unnatural words: had the builders of the tower of Babel whistled while they worked, the history (and legend!) of the world would be entirely different to that we know today.

"It is more than adequate." Dolores le Grande, was damning with faint praise; but her verdict might have been more severe had the song not been by, and for, another member of the Heredias clan.

"What the heck have you been walking in?" I looked at J.C.'s feet. The once light-blue track shoes were black with some foul slime.

"Old sump oil," Jesús said. "Some *tonto* must have done a service job up here."

The stench was so powerful I could no longer smell the pines which the heat of the sun, following a recent shower, had set to perfuming the whole area. "For goodness sake, go and get them cleaned up," I told him. They were words which I would later live to regret.

The crowd was thickest near the church doors, as the newly-weds came forth with the colourful congregation. Ana, a mere sixteen years of age, petite and light skinned, wore a simple white satin gown, embroidered with tiny pink pearls, the tulle veil falling like dove wings from a crown of pink pearls. If she was fearful of the *gitano* ceremony to come, her face did not show it, only the tightness of the knuckles of her left hand as she held Honorio's arm suggested her uncertainty with what lay ahead. Several girls were trying to get Ana's attention by gathering up their skirts and stamping their way through a *buleria* or a *sevillana.* Friends shouted encouragement as the dancers, laughing and flushed in their polka dot dresses got lost in the crowd. The bridal couple were led to a clearing in the trees where there was an apple-wood fire, round which stood the *gitano* elders who were soon joined by the bride and groom's *padrinos.* As they assembled, the night air was filled with the throbbing of guitars. Now Ana and Honorio took up their positions. Declarations of loyalty to the community and to each other were led by the elders in the Romany tongue. I heard *sida** mentioned, and hoped this meant the couple were virus free; but I was too far away to hear, or see, in detail. I did see the flashing of steel as the boy's left arm, and the girl's right arm, were held by their *padrino* while an elder drew a blade across the inside of each wrist. The blood spurted over the front of Ana's satin bridal gown before a long white scarf bound boy and girl together, blood to blood, love to love, life to death.

"How utterly revolting!"

I wasn't sure if the remark made by the Mrs Porky Legs standing next to me was intended for my private approval, or the world at large; but as I thoroughly disagreed with her sentiments, I told her so in no uncertain terms.

"I am quite familiar with your programme," she said. "In fact, I have shares in Radio Independiente Plus." Then, preening herself like a twenty-year-old, she added majestically, "I'm one of the directors wives."

---

*Aids

"*Señora,*" I said, "I don't care if you're the director's only wife. I still think it's a superb piece of traditional drama. This sad old world is in urgent need of some romantic passion." It was as I said it, that I saw some romantic passion going on not far from where I was standing.

J.C. was seated on the stump of a felled tree. Several young men his own age were gathered round. Kneeling at his feet was a woman of indeterminate age, engrossed in whatever it was she was doing. A pungent smell was drifting from the group, dominating the smell of pine, of apple-wood, even J.C.'s much-travelled socks. It was unmistakably some manufactured perfume, or toilet water, and as I approached, I could see a large, expensive-looking bottle. It was empty. The label read expensively, too: 'Chanel No. 5'. The young woman appeared to have used the entire contents to wash J.C.'s shoes and feet, and rid them of the oil in which he had been stabbling.

"You're a fool, Jesús," one of his companions said. "Don't you know she's a whore. It's going to cost you."

"She's been carrying that bottle of froggie pong about for years. It's about the only thing she's got," another said.

"The only thing she's *had,* " laughed a third. "How're you going to keep your pussy sweet now, Dol?"

I felt suddenly embarrassed by the scene and walked away. One of J.C.'s companions followed me. "Who is she?" I asked.

"Don't you know old Dolores Madelein? I thought everyone knew her. Cheapest bit of home comfort this side of Almeria."

When J.C. joined me some time later, I knew I would have to choose words carefully. "You're smelling and looking much sweeter," I said. "But isn't she a bit old for you?"

"There is no age in eternity," Jesús said.

"But her lifestyle . . . ."

"Our father made all men equal," Jesús said. "The evil men do made us different."

"But J.C., surely you didn't need to let her show off like that. It was very expensive perfume."

"It was all she had that she could call her own, and she

wanted to give it to me," he replied. "How can I say no to love?"

I was about to argue, but what with? Mere words were useless against such total conviction as J.C. possessed. As it was, I filed in the back of my mind the fact that J.C. now had two Dolores dominating his life – his mother and . . . his lover?

Jugs of wine and trays of *chorizo* and *salchichon tapas* were being passed round to refresh the guests. A shout went up that the *juntadora* had arrived, and a tall, thin woman whose age I estimated to be about fifty and whose sober dress would not have been out of place in a court of law, was shepherded by Carla and several other women to a tent set up for her purpose some distance from the apple-wood fire. That purpose (or art, mystery, quackery or downright hocus-pocus) is the ancient *gitano* rite of *prueba de pañuelo* by which is established the virginity (or otherwise) of the bride. Payment appeared to be strictly in advance: the only man allowed near the oracle was the father of the bride, and I saw him with a bundle of 5,000 pts. bank-notes, counting out at least ten before the clawing hand was satisfied. Only then was Ana led by her bridesmaids into the presence of the *juntadora*.

Raucous laughter came from two long trestle tables at which Douggie Hardman was entertaining the international wine writers. An American woman with hair that trailed onto her neighbour's soup plate, was telling broad jokes in an even broader Bronx accent. "And then there was the Greek boy who left home because he didn't like the way his father was rearing him."

Mari-Carmen and Pippa had found seats at the end of the table nearest me. "Pedro," my producer asked, "what is so funny about a Greek boy leaving home?"

"It isn't funny," I told her. "And the lady isn't a lady."

She must have noticed me looking at Pippa's ear-rings, simple but stylish pieces of precious metal wire patterned and, I had no doubt, sold by *gitanos*, because she abruptly told Pippa to go make a telephone call – here of all places – and when she had gone, patted the empty seat and urged me to sit and talk. She pretended she wanted to talk about the ear-rings, the fact that Pippa had returned the diamond rings to her would be sugar daddy, John Truscott. But what she really wanted me to know was that Pippa had made up her mind at last to 'come out'.

"We're going to buy a little place of our own in Velez," she said. "It's quite old and needs a lot of work done on it. We can do it a bit at a time. And it's *ours*."

"Good for you," I said. "That calls for a celebration. Has friend Douggie got any champers we can open?"

"There's a problem with his wine," Mari-Carmen said,lowering her voice and looking about her anxiously for fear of being overheard. "He's brought all these media people with him and a new boy at the bodega thought he was referring to a new table water *con gas* when he asked for six cases of bubbly." She gave me a wry smile. "He should be more precise with Spanish staff."

"How many Spaniards call it *cava*, as European law says they should? I don't, do you?"

"The French are . . . *terrible* . . . *mauvais* . . . "

I was about to agree with her on all counts, but I saw Pippa returning from her enforced telephone call. "I'll leave you two love birds to enjoy the wedding breakfast," I told her as I made my escape.

The *juntadora* had opened her tent. One of the *gitano* elders had escorted the father of the groom and the father of the bride to see the proof of virginity. A crowd of women were in the tent, swaying, hand clapping and singing. Passing from hand to hand was a large white cotton handkerchief, tied in three peaks with coloured ribbons and rosettes, giving the blood stains the maximum dramatic impact. Now the proof was passed out to the *padrinos* and then to the guests. Everyone began to sing as the bride appeared. *"Jelli, jelli, jelli"* wailed the chorus. It was almost Arab in its complex modulations; but when I asked what the song was, nobody seemed to know. "It's always sung at Romany weddings," was as far as I got.

The crowd began to move away from the tent as a tray of food and wine was taken in to revive the (presumably) exhausted *juntadora*. But the bride's ordeal was far from over. Eager hands hoisted her onto the shoulders of Honorio's *padrino* who lurched with her in the direction of the much-painted storehouse, closely followed by Ana's *padrino* carrying her groom. As they entered the hall there was a great roar of welcome and a hail of pink and white sugared almonds as bride and groom were danced shoulder high over the concrete floor, faster, faster and still faster, the whole time being showered with almonds thrown from the pockets of satin wedding aprons worn by many of the female guests. And risking life and limb, the children scrambled like wild animals to collect the sweetmeats from the dusty floor before they were crushed under the dancers' feet. Someone estimated that fifty kilos of the good-luck nuts had taken flight; but the luck only burst free with every snap-and-crack of the mass *zapateado*. Ana's younger brother, Ricardo, reached out and grasped his brother-in-law's shirt, ripping it off his body in one violent movement. This was the signal for a score of eager hands to rip off every male shirt they could find. I decided to leave before the dance degenerated into an orgy.

Several men, I noticed, had anticipated the affront to male dignity and had brought spare shirts with them. Outside, in the fresh air, I nearly knocked over J.C.'s mum, or rather, she nearly knocked over me.

"Peter, I *must* talk to you," she said. "I've always tried to bring up my family as Christians. Perhaps I've tried too hard where Jesús is concerned. I can understand youthful high spirits, particularly as he is an only child, but tonight he's gone much too far with his pranks."

"Pranks?" I thought at first that mum had met up with the other Dolores, but this sounded infinitely more serious.

"Everybody's talking about it. He's turned water into wine!"

"If he can do that, I'm opening a bar tomorrow!"

"Please be serious," she said. "He may need medical help of some kind."

"Like da Vinci needed medical help to paint the Mona Lisa, Beethoven needed medical help to compose the

Pastoral symphony, or Donne needed medical help to write his sonnets?"

"Please, oh, *please* be serious!"

"I am serious. And frightened. If humanity can put a young girl through the kind of ordeal Ana has been put through tonight, all because for Honorio's honour he must wed a virgin, I dread to think what humanity can do to a boy who turns water into wine."

I left her to the not so tender mercy of the other guests who, recognizing her as the famous le Grande Dolores, hoped they would get a free performance from her by calling for a song. I went in search of Mari-Carmen, hoping to get an unbiased report on the 'miracle'.

"We all thought it a delightful little wine. So light and sparkling after the heavy red we'd been drinking," she said.

"But was it table water *con gas*, or was it wine?" I insisted.

"It tasted all right to us, didn't it, Pippa?"

I went over to the van where Douggie Hardman was checking his stock. Remembering my interview with the man some time back, I knew I'd have to be careful. "There's a story going round, Mr Hardman, that some of your mineral water was turned into wine. Can you give me the facts, please?"

He was all charm, which surprised me. "Just a label confusion at the bottling plant, old chap. The only miracle about it is that we can retail it in the U.K. for less than three quid a bottle."

"So you don't believe the story that's got around?"

"Not this story." He hesitated. "But that doesn't mean I don't believe every word the Good Book says."

I went in search of J.C. but failed to find him, either in the dance hall or among the couples doing their thing together under the moon and pines. So I assumed he'd make his own way home; one of his teenage hangers-on was sure to have transport. When I got back to the apartment myself, I was surprised to find him waiting for me with the best morning-after pick-you-up in the world . . .

a clear glass jug, sweating with ice, brimming with fresh orange juice and champagne.

"Delicious!" I said, draining the glass.

"What do you think's in it?" Jesús asked.

"Orange juice and champers. What else?"

"Orange juice and Mr Hardman's new table water, *con gas.*"

"No alcohol?"

"No alcohol, Mister Peter."

One thing was certain. I wasn't going to take up his mum's suggestion that he sought medical advice.

ROMERIA DEL ROCIO

THE DAY FRANCO died . . . there was no crime: you could walk the streets, day or night, without fear of being mugged: or park your unlocked car and return to it an hour, or twenty-four hours, later to find car and contents exactly as you left them. The day Franco died . . . Spain was a country of strict morality: a friend and I, going to bathe before breakfast in the then tiny fishing village of Fuengirola, were led away from a deserted beach by two Guardia Civil officers because we removed the clothes we were wearing *over* our swimming costumes. The day Franco died . . . cement being in short supply, its proportion in concrete decreased as the proportion of sand increased, so that tourist hotels fell down as fast as they were going up. The day Franco died . . . everybody went to church: the priest in all things material was more powerful than God, for upon his nod or disapproval depended a job, a house, a permit, a passport, a hope; the Sunday *paseo* was a social obligation and the possession of a Sunday suit could transcend the pangs of hunger. The day Franco died . . . Jesús was born: and like all his contemporaries had to cope with a world of rapid change – from abacus to computer in half a generation, frantically abandoning the old, uncritically adopting the new – from psychadellic drugs to sexual deviation, with only will-power and wellies for protection. It is not so much the survival of the fittest, rather, who survives at all in the manner the maker of man intended. Jesús Cepillo Herẹdias is a survivor. He understands eternity. The day Jesús was born . . . Franco died: and the evil he did, stays died with him.

It was Dolores le Grande's idea that the family should reunite to join the annual *romeria* to E1 Rocio, which she had done many times in her youth, but had not attempted again since Jesús was born. She said it would get him away from too much public exposure: it was one thing to be a performing artiste like herself and quite another to be the subject of tabloid newspaper headlines, as was her son.

The latest of these came from a meeting of the society of vintners, who were demanding a pledge from this *vagabundo* that he would cease forthwith turning water into wine. All the same, I couldn't help feeling that J.C.'s mum was convinced that I was the root cause of her son's youthful peccadilloes: she was supremely confident that a *romeria* would point him in the right direction. She was not to know that, as we set out for seven days of ecstatic devotion, pagan revelry and fearful fanaticism, it was to be the beginning of the end: or, as J.C. was to put it some time later, the end of the beginning.

Nearly a million *gitanos* are on the move across Europe once a year, every year, heading for Spain, for Andalusia, for the most western province of Huelva, for the tiny white hamlet on the marshes known as El Rocio – Our Lady of the Dew – in order to worship a little image known also as La Blanca Paloma (The White Dove). This vast army of reverent revellers is first marshalled in the principal cities throughout Andalusia – Almeria, Cadiz, Cordoba, Granada, Huelva, Jaen, Málaga and Seville – where they are grouped into *hermandades*. We started our pilgrimage from Málaga with early morning mass said at the parish church of La Purisima to the sound of the first festive rockets. We travelled on foot, on donkey, on horseback, on trailers and tractors, land rovers and oxen carts, old and new caravans, everyone and everything decorated by man's unique imagination. And to a background of pilgrim song, the rhythmic clapping of hands, and the incessant woossshhh! as rocket after rocket took flight, the procession slowly crossed the city and set off down the glorious golden road.

> * *"Olé! . . . olé!, olé!, olé!, olé! . . .*
> *Al Rocio yo quiero volver*
> *pa'cantarle a la Virgen con fe*
> *con un olé! . . ."*

---

*"Bravo! . . . etc. To Rocio I'm going, to sing to the Virgin with faith and a bravo!"

The focus of all this passionate devotion is a small carved statue that, so the story goes, turned up in a hollow tree during the reign of Alfonso the Wise, six centuries ago. It was discovered by a shepherd who attempted to carry it to his village; but he stopped to have a rest, and fell asleep. By the time he awoke, the Virgin had vanished. He went back to the hollow tree – and there she was, exactly as he had first found her! She has never been moved again since then. As her fame spread and miracles were associated with her, the sanctuary became a place of pilgrimage.

"They're always changing things," Dolores said, looking down on a terrace of white *cal* and red geranium covered houses. Our convoy had come to a temporary halt while an oxen-drawn farm wagon was disentangled from a couple of builder's skips. "They won't be there when we come back in a week's time."

José, J.C.'s father, whose head was almost a perfectly shaped oval, so much so that he resembled an olive that had stayed in the sun too long, shouted from the driving seat of the tractor pulling our caravan, "You shouldn't complain about progress!"

"You're confusing progress with change," Jesús said. "What does it profit man if he builds a paradise and lives in it like bedlam?" And with that, he effectively stifled any further family conversation. I felt a social, cultural, and intellectual gulf opening up between us, like that which can exist between parents and children who have won scholarships to higher education; and which seldom exists between parents and children whose higher education is simply purchased with daddy's dough-ray-me. Such subtlety was lost on our fellow travellers – the grandfather (who had to be persuaded that his much-travelled *caracol* would never make the journey); an uncle (who had traded a pair of fighting cocks for the temporary use of the owner's travelling cockpit, viz. the caravan); and the elderly parents of Dolores's fruit-grower neighbour in Alora (who conveniently wasn't going to need the tractor, but hadn't the time to make the pilgrimage himself).

The uncle wanted to know if there were any cock fights

in England and when I told him they were against the law, together with dog fights and bull fights seemed genuinely dismayed. "I thought England was a democracy, like Spain," he said. "Maybe that's why so many English come to live here permanently."

We were passing a typical urbanization as he spoke. It looked more like a film set than a place for comfortable living. It is a fact that the Spanish themselves mostly live in the capital and leave the ghetto, or the Costa as it is more politely known, to the *extranjeros*, who from atop Gibralfaro can be seen as so many sheep waiting to be fleeced. If the city holds no charm for him, the Spaniard moves east – to a chalet in Palo, or a quiet country retreat near Velez, or Frigiliana.

J.C. must have been reading my thoughts. "Are they dull because they're respectable, or respectable because they're dull?" he asked.

"That's not a very nice thing to say, dear," his mother chided. "*We're* foreign to foreigners."

"Nice, nice, NICE! You don't understand. None of you understand!" Jesús said. There was an adult anger in his eyes I had never seen before. "They all want to remain as they are because not one of them wants to hear a new idea."

"That's enough for now, dear," his mother warned. "We're here to enjoy ourselves."

"Listen, mother, LISTEN!" Jesús cried. He stood there, arms spread wide, as though embracing the whole world, as José drove the caravan slowly in convoy through the crowd gathered to see us on our way. And thus, J.C. delivered his sermon on the *montes*.

"All you worry about is making money, being a success, being admired – by *nice* people! You'd look like white tombstones if it wasn't for your suntans. You think so much of yourselves, but each one of us is of no greater or no lesser worth to our father. The more you grab, the less you have. If your life is spent worrying about things, instead of people, how can you be ready to make that great journey into the unknown?" He was magnificent, exuding a wild and passionate innocence with every word. The flamboyant giving of gifts, the pretence at charity while helping oneself, was no help to anyone. "Who are these people who want to judge others? Who want to be a Member of Parliament, a business *jefe*, a man of affairs, or something equally as tedious?" he asked, his voice rising as the crowd in the street began moving with the caravan so as not to miss his every word, growing larger by the minute as it did so. "Indeed, they will become what they want to become. That is their punishment, that is their mill stone . . . that is their cross. But I say unto you, live for now! LIVE FOR LIFE! L I V E F O R L- O – V – E !!"

The crowd jostling for position round the caravan burst into spontaneous applause. One man fell to his knees in prayer and immediately a dozen fell over him. In the mêlée that ensued, José was able to speed up the departure and the crowd, unable to maintain the pace, dispersed, and was gone.

"You've done it now, J.C.," I told him. "Point of no return."

"Pull yourself together, boy," the uncle wheezed through the fire and brimstone of what he called his *pipa del campo*. "It's not manly. All religion's superstitious stuff for women."

Gramps was too old in the tooth to stoke a family dispute by risking a point of view; but he did say, "Don't let them bully you, Jesús. Stick to your guns, lad, and say only what you know to be true and you can't go wrong."

But J.C. went very wrong. The convoy marshal called a comfort stop and all the vehicles in our section pulled into the side of the road. José got down from the driving seat of the tractor and immediately approached J.C., anger written all over his tight-skinned face, so much anger that words seemed to pour out of him before there was any movement of the lips.

"How dare you behave like that in front of your mother! We came on this *romeria* for her sake, not yours! No son of mine will behave in this manner, is that clear?"

"I am no son of yours," Jesús said.

I felt the electricity in the air. It swept down the back of my neck and gave me goose pimples in the heat of the day.

José stood there, unable to get out words at all, his body rigid and trembling like an old man with the palsy.

"If you aren't my son, then whose son are you?" José managed to get out at last.

"I am the son of our father," Jesús said.

"Liar! Blasphemer!" José's whole face was distorted with rage as he struggled to find words that expressed what was boiling over inside him. "Get away from me! I never want to see you again! Out of my sight. Away! Beelzebub! Be gone!"

For a moment, I thought I was in a scene from grand opera instead of standing in the shade of a magnificent old caravan on the side of the road, somewhere between Málaga and Cadiz. Then J.C. reached out and grasped me by the shoulder.

"It's best you come with us, Mister Peter," he said. "I will protect you for ever."

"Protect, J.C.. From what are you going to protect me?"

"You don't know these people like I do. Many of them have the devil in them. They cohabit with all that is evil."

"On a *romeria*?"

"Even on a *romeria*."

I'd promised Mari-Carmen a full report on the pilgrimage to El Rocio. I'd never yet failed on any assignment since the days I was a cub reporter. Technically, J.C. was breaking the rules of his probation; but I had no inclination to get involved now in the legal niceties of what was right and what was wrong. All round me the *rocieros* were beginning to pour out the *fino*. What was I supposed to do if I was to follow this strange young man and his little band of disciples? Put on sackcloth and ashes and wander the wilderness of the Guadalquivir estuary?

"As I told you, point of no return, J.C.. I go my way. You go yours."

He reached into the caravan and pulled out a bed-roll and what looked like a wedge of soda bread, gave me a shy little smile, and the next moment was gone, melting into the crowd of travellers and their lookers-on.

"I don't understand what's happened to him," José said when he had quelled some of his rage, "You watch your kids grow up. You don't expect them to be perfect but . . . first drugs and now some kind of religious mania. Do you think they are connected in any way?"

"There's no proof he's been pushing drugs and I'm as certain as one can be in these matters he doesn't use any himself." I was trying to clear my mind of all the mumbo-jumbo I'd ever heard, or read, about religious mania. "There doesn't seem to be anything manic about his behaviour. He doesn't go around trying to form yet another religious sect, either for a financial rip off or as a kinky self-made Messiah."

"Every day he seems to get involved in something that gets into the newspapers. His mother may not show it, but she's worried sick by his behaviour. We *gitanos* have enough trouble from them that wishes we were wiped off the face of the earth, without all these so-called miracles."

"He doesn't claim to perform miracles," I said. "It's just that things seem to happen when J.C.'s around. He's young and he loves life. Maybe there's no more to it than that."

"When people want to pay good money for any of his old clothes, I think there is more to it than that," José said.

"Are you serious?"

"I'm not a liar! Two days ago a man gave me five thousand pesetas for a pair of his old jeans. They were only two thousand in the *rastro* when they were new. Now why should a man do a thing like that?"

The fetish ads. in the columns of the gay press flashed through my mind. "Maybe they think a fly-button a good enough talisman to ward off everything from the *gripe* to *sida*."

"I don't like it. It has to stop," the father said. "It's making me look a fool."

I was about to tell him I didn't think J.C. was stoppable when the convoy marshal signalled us back on the road and José had to run for his tractor. For the next few hours the going was easy and I sat on the rear steps of the caravan, soaking up the sunshine and trying to make up my mind if J.C. had miraculous powers, or whether he was just a healthy teenager with a magnetic personality and a laudable desire to help people. I still hadn't made up my mind when we came to the Guadalquivir estuary, a few kilometres west of the 'sherry' shipping centre of Sanlucar de Barrameda. Several *hermandades* were already queuing up on the sands. In their tight, short jackets and leather chaps, the 'brothers' looked as arrogant as the tightly-reined horses stamping their hoof-prints in the sand. Gleaming horse-drawn carriages were arriving every minute as cries of *'Viva!'* greeted the arrival of every *simpecado*, a portrait of the Virgin, lavishly presented by each *hermandad* on its leading vehicle. Our Virgin was mounted in an elaborate, lily-festooned silver float. The Spanish *armada* was there with landing craft to help the pilgrims make the crossing. Asses and mules kicked their protests at being craned by belly-sling. Horses, their nerves contained by bloodied bits as bridles strained to breaking point, were shying, rearing, and defying the rider's control. On the far side of the river, the *hermandades* reformed. Bottles of *fino* were passed from hand to hand. Girls in vivid polka dot dresses flounced their frills and rode side-saddle behind macho boy friends.

As the sun set, convoy after convoy of the motley procession pulled into any patch of grassland they could find. Tomorrow would be a gruelling day under a remorseless sun, pushing west over shifting sand, marsh and pine forest. Suddenly the *romeria* became a picnic, as families set up tents, tables, chairs, ice boxes, cutlery, glasses. Nets of fresh shellfish seemingly appeared from nowhere, washed down with the golden liquid produced in the enchanted triangle formed by Jerez de la Frontera, Puerto de Santa Maria and Sanlucar de Barrameda. The beat of drums and the whistle of flutes startled nature as the *tamborileros*, who accompany the pilgrims, sang and made music for the dance until everyone was too exhausted to do anything but drop to the most comfortable spot they could find . . . and sleep.

Come the dawn and the first convoy was on its way before the sun fingered with flame-red light the trail we had made the previous day. We started moving through groves of eucalyptus and pine; then the dunes, and vehicle after vehicle was quickly bogged down. Engines overheated and had to be cooled. If it was savage for the mules, it was even worse for the highly-strung horses. Scores of them were bleeding from nose and mouth. Several died. One *rociero* told me frankly, and let me record him saying it, that he never brought his best horses for the pilgrimage. He would be lucky if three out of five returned. We were passing through one of the great European nature reserves, the Coto Doñana; but there was precious little sign of wild life. Rabbit, deer and lynx had all fled before the noise of our engines. It was near midnight before our day ended. We saw the welcoming light of camp fires near the Coto Doñana Palace, a hunting lodge for more than three centuries and now a biological research station. The next morning I was woken by Dolores with a mug of black coffee laced with anise (though I'd swear it was the other way about).

"They say thousands have left the convoys by foot and have gone off north towards Seville, following my Jesús." Her face was a mass of mosquito bites, as was mine, and I wanted to say something like, "Let's enumerate them," but I knew she was much too worried for jokes. "No good can come of it," she went on. "He is behaving as though he's possessed by some evil spirit."

"Why evil?" I asked.

"Well, it can't be right. No one else behaves like he does. They'll put him back in jail for certain. City life doesn't agree with him. I should have kept him in Alora with me."

"I can assure you that if he is possessed by anything, it's certainly not evil," I told her. "At worst, some of his enthusiasm needs to be throttled back a bit. Don't worry. And don't listen to rumours. He may well be in E1 Rocio already, waiting our arrival."

"I hope you're right," Dolores said. I hoped I was right, too.

Shortly after midday the sanctuary itself appeared, a dazzling white wedding cake affair soaring above the marshes. For most of the year the orderly lines of houses on either side of it were unoccupied, but now it was as alive as a colony of ants, with some fifty thousand *hermandades* setting up temporary homes, plus hundreds of thousands of independent pilgrims pouring in by bus and car, motor-cycle and pedal-cycle, anything that would get them there on time for their date with the little Virgin. The dirt streets were congested with an excess of humanity as the iron bells of El Rocio clanged their welcome. The smell of barbecued chicken mixed with the acrid smoke from the fried onion smothering the hot dogs, dominated the smell of jasmine. A little *gitana* appeared to have cornered the jasmine market, maybe because with every sale she would pause to give the customer a barefoot dance of undisputed authenticity. You could buy a plastic snake or a tatty plaster Virgin, and a hopeful Moroccan was trying to flog 'all silver, feel the weight' Mexican coins. You'd need a hundred thousand Spanish pesetas to rent a house for a day and to have a sleeping bag in a corner, ten thousand. Money flowed like quicksilver in El Rocio. You want to buy a horse? Hire a woman? Sleep with my son? ('No, I only do it standing up: it's effeminate to do it laying down.') You want Scotch whisky? Only ten thousand . . . eight . . . only . . . only . . .

"I haven't found Jesús yet," Dolores said, squeezing into the already over-full caravan. "I have a feeling in my bones that something's not right."

"I have the same feeling," gramps said. "And it's the anise."

I couldn't help feeling the Spanish wished I wasn't there while they tried to come to terms with what were confusing events for us all, so I excused myself on the pretext that I needed to stretch my legs before turning in for the night. It must have been nearly midnight that I found myself in front of the sanctuary. Behind an iron grille, the tiny image of the Virgin, doll-like in her crisp new robes, looked down on the fornicating faithful. Those not engaged in some orgiastic exercise looked up in awe, crossing themselves, praying, or just staring at her as tears ran down their cheeks. Somewhere in the crowd I heard English voices. I caught the word 'miracle' and then a man's voice, "He's better value than this crappy lot." I felt sure they were talking about J.C..

"Who's that speaking English? Please, I want to talk to you," I said.

They were Australian, three in all, two boys and a girl; or it may have been two girls and a boy.

"What can we do for you, matey?" the tallest one asked. He had a complexion that showed every sign of never having taken kindly to the sun.

"Do you come from the lot that went off on their own?"

"There's no law that says we have to stay here, is there? You're not *another* Spanish pig, are you?"

"I'm a radio journalist."

"Is there a difference?" the one of undetermined sex asked.

I ignored the remark. "I want to know what's going on."

"For free? Or are you paying?" It was the third of the unholy trinity that put the question, a young woman who wouldn't stop fixing me with her Bette Davis eyes.

"I don't have cash with me," I said. "But you can apply for a fee if any of your material is used." I didn't add that they had a cat-in-hell chance of squeezing anything out of Tio Mac.

"There's this crazy guy out there who calls himself Jesús," the tall one of the three said. "Everyone seems to think he works miracles. You know, tricks. Like the things the priests read out from the Bible."

"And are they tricks?"

The big guy grinned. "Of course they are, matey. There's a trick to every trade, isn't there?"

"You're accusing him of deliberate deceit," I said.

"A lot of people out there believe they work," the undetermined one said. "He smeared some mud over a blind girl's eyes and she saw for the first time in her life."

"He merely washed the cow's face," the bulbous-eyed one explained. "She hadn't washed for a month of monthlies."

They all giggled like schoolgirls and began arguing if the patient was, or was not, genuinely blind. A consensus seemed impossible to reach, so the undetermined one summed up with, "She said it was a miracle and she should know."

"Well, it will be a bloody miracle if the bloke can feed all five thousand on one piece of soda bread and a half-eaten tin can of sardines," the tall one said.

"He was using the can to show us how to collect cactus fruit." The undetermined one gave me a smile of encouragement, such as is given to the elderly or simple-minded. "It was really quite clever. All we had to do was find a can – and we eat."

I decided I wasn't going to get any more useful information concerning J.C.'s present whereabouts and whatabouts, and left them arguing among themselves. How he was, or was not, feeding five thousand followers in the uninhabited scrub land of the Guadalquivir estuary would become a part of local history (or folk-lore) I had no doubt. J.C. had once shown me how to gather cactus fruit, which he sold in the market. All that one needed was a length of sugar cane such as the old women use to *cal* their houses, an empty sharp-edged can, some espato grass to bind cane and can together . . . and the knack of flicking the wrist to encase the spiky fruit in the can and snap it free of the plant. I had never acquired this knack. Had I done so, fumble-fingers that I am, I would have regarded it as a miracle. A minor miracle, nothing as lavish as J.C. seemed embarked upon, but a miracle nevertheless.

"Viva la Blanca Paloma!" the cry went up.

It was the following morning and the *hermandades* were each taking turns to pay homage to the Virgin, starting with Almonte, the nearest town to Rocio: they organize the *romeria* and control the sanctuary. After each homage regional anthems were played and sung, rockets launched and bells rung. All day long the faithful took communion, said confession, joined the dancing and the drinking and the fornication. The sheer energy being generated and expended was formidable. Barmen were working non-stop for the best part of a week: and the mosquitoes were scarcely less active, even getting at me when, so often in the past, Paul had joked I was naturally repulsive enough to keep them at bay. Our winged tormentors thrived on the anise with which high octane fuel hardened *rocieros* kept going. By sunset, it was all I could do to stand. Adding to my predicament, I was constantly being importuned by sex obsessed humanity (which sex, mattered not to anyone). We all looked and, I guess, felt at our worst. For some illogical reason I couldn't get out of my mind a gay soiree in Chelsea in my youth, when I'd embarrassed myself, if not my host, by delivering a conversation stopper with, "I've never been to bed with an ugly boy: but I've woken up with quite a few." And then I began thinking about J.C.. Why hadn't we slept together? His mum expected it, otherwise why the gift of a patchwork bed-cover . . . for a double bed! Was it because of something inherently moral in me? Or something so innocent and pure in him? The thought of J.C., those steady, kind, but piercing eyes that saw right through to my soul, was enough to make me flay out with my arms to repel two dark skinned youngsters, one with an erection fully exposed, who were trying playfully to pull me towards a pile of dirty cushions. As one of them pressed hot, rough-skinned lips against my cheeks, a gut-turning roar began rolling across the vast crowd like an ocean wave. It was some moments before I realized what was happening, The protective fence had been broken and the perpetrators had seized the Virgin.

"Viva la Blanca Paloma! Viva!"

No one knew which *hermandad* was responsible for the outrage. We could see the Virgin held aloft on her dais at a crazy angle. She looked as intoxicated as her devotees, rocking wildly as she was born from the sanctuary on young shoulders. Several groups were struggling now for the right to carry her. The atmosphere was ecstatic. All kinds of flowers (and some vegetables) were thrown at her by the surging spectators. Women were struggling with the triumphant bearers to get near enough to touch the dais. A mother lifted her baby from a carry-cot and held it aloft like a swaddled plum duff, to be passed from hand to hand over the heads of the crowd till the screaming infant had made contact with the rocking effigy of the blessed virgin and was safely handled back again to the rightful owner. Now we could see the Virgin's captors, a tough mob in military fatigues; but they were soon tiring of the struggle and an even tougher mob dived in to rescue the Virgin, *their* Virgin. It was more than alcohol that kept them going: they were exalted, possessed. "I touched her! I touched her!!" a woman screamed triumphantly, tears trickling down her bruised and blooded face.

"Guapa! Guapa! Bonita! Bonita!"

The magnificent multitude was marching as it rejoiced and sang. And Nuestra Senora del Rocio, La Blanca Paloma, Queen of the Marshes, zigzagged into a purple dawn. All day she was processed to every visiting *hermandad* and there, before the brothers' *simpecado*, listened to priestly praise, prayers, and peptic cries of "Viva!" The swooning faithful were revived with the remains of *fino*, anise, beer, whisky, gin, even urine (said to be more than a hundred percent proof), till at last the sacred shrine swayed back into her sanctuary.

When I returned to the caravan I found Dolores alone in the gathering darkness, in tears; "Jesús has sent me a message by one of his friends," she gasped. "He's not going to join us for the journey home. We only came on the *romeria* because of him . . . I wanted to do something to keep the family . . . together."

"What's he going to do?"

"Everyone has come away from that dreadful wilderness except him. He's out there alone. They say he intends to stay there alone for forty days and forty nights."

"What the devil for?" I was rapidly losing patience with J.C.'s antics; but a moment later I wished I hadn't mentioned the devil.

"He says he has to be tempted," the mother cried.

"Why?"

"The boy who brought the message described it as a trial of strength. Like an army survival course."

"Then let us pray he survives," I said. I thought I knew what J.C. was up to, he had often spoken to me of the need for solitude, time to see ourselves as others see us: but I decided not to confuse his mother's frantic mind any more than it was already confused. It is depressing to realize how few people know themselves before they die, know their souls for what they are. How few of us ever do anything on our own accord. It is quite true. Most of us are someone else – we accept someone else's thoughts, someone else's opinions, copy their dress styles, mimic their eating habits, even attempt to duplicate their passions. A young man whose mother had had baptized, Jesús, and who I knew as J.C., was living in our world, aware as few people are aware, that he is, was, and will be unique. Love he has for the poor, for those confined in jail, for the lowly, for the wretched: but with compassion more powerful even than the light of high noon, he pities the rich, the selfish, the mean, and all who waste the freedom of their unique being by becoming slaves to *things*.

As the *rocieros* departed for another year, the little Blanca Paloma was returned to her shrine. Beneath her golden mantle and six white petticoats the Virgin is said to consist of a couple of pieces of box-wood. Only her official dresser knows: those who may never know, keep the faith.

. . . y el viejo pudiese*

I'D SPENT A MONTH in hell worrying about J.C. and the consequences of his having gone missing. Thanks to Mari-Carmen, daily announcements were put out by the Spanish language service of Radio Independiente Plus in the hope he may hear one and respond by getting in touch. But no response came. I felt utterly alone, drained of life. I cleaned the apartment every morning like a robot, numbed, and indifferent to every action. It wasn't till well into the third week that I realized I wasn't cleaning J.C.'s room. I wasn't even putting a hand on the door-knob. As Paul used to say, every time one parts one dies a little: and as the days went by, I became more and more convinced that I was not going to see J.C. again except in a coffin. The whole world was grey. Nothing made sense; and the nonsensical, became logical. So I wasn't the least surprised walking into my usual elevenses cafeteria to find Teresa,the blind ONCE ticket seller, no longer on her usual rush-woven chair in the shade of the canopy. In her place was a young man reading *Marca*, with Teresa's notice at his feet: CIEGA. I was about to give him a mouthful of words that just might be mightier than the sword, when I saw the dog sitting by his side. I was still going to give the bastard a mouthful, but I bit my tongue in time. The dog had advanced cataract of both eyes. Black Spain became just that little less black.

Don Luis had been on the phone every hour of every day, wanting to know if I'd had any communication of any kind from J.C.. The old lawyer's professional reputation was at stake for having sworn before a notary that J.C. was

---

**Si el mozo supiese y el viejo pudiese, no habria cosa que no se hiciese.*(If the young man knew how and the old man was able, there would be nothing which wouldn't be done).

[Spanish proverb]

without blame in the drugs hassle that had landed him in court; his friendship with the judge who released J.C. from jail, on the strength of the boy's promises to behave, was in jeopardy; his future contacts with *extranjeros* like myself would be nil, in view of my inability to carry out the court's requirements; and if all that wasn't enough, his wife had found out he was trying to sell the family Picasso – and he had yet to tell her its origin was far from authenticated.

"I've persuaded them to put him on the missing persons list, as you suggested. Not that they'll do much about it."

"Good", I said. "It's better than a kick in the teeth."

"It won't be good for him if they pick him up."

"At least he'll be safe and have a proper meal!"

"In all probability they'll put him back in jail."

"Why the hell should they? He hasn't committed a crime. The boy's just a little mixed up. I was, at his age."

"They think he's . . . how do you say it? . . . cocking a snook at them. They'll almost certainly have public opinion behind them. You know the extent of the hostility there is towards *gitanos*."

"And *maricóns*, Moroccans, and one-arm bandits! Surely, Don Luis, with your vast experience of life, you don't give a damn for public opinion,"

"In the end, we all have to," he said.

Don Luis hadn't been off the line more than ten seconds before Mari-Carmen was on.

"I've been trying to get you all day, Pedro," she said.

"You've got me."

It sounded as though she was in the cutting room, editing tapes. "Tio Mac had me in his office as soon as he arrived – "

"I thought he was too old for jiggy-jiggy."

I almost heard her blush. "You are *awful!*"

"You used to be his personal secretary, didn't you?"

"Not that kind!" There was an interruption on the line and I heard her say to someone, in Spanish, not to change the label on the spool, as it wasn't her fault the *zarzuela* programme had been wiped. "Listen, this is very serious. He told me he doesn't want any more announcements made about Jesús on the Spanish language service."

"Why not?"

"Pippa thinks one of his cronies has been getting at him on the moral issue."

"What moral issue?"

"You know he doesn't approve of your life style."

"It's not *me* that's gone AWOL!"

"He takes everything so personally." There was a crash in the background and her voice was momentarily lost. When it returned, she was saying " . . . another wiped tape, damn it! Pedro, I have to ring off now. We'll put our heads together in the morning."

"If you say so." I wanted to talk some more, but she'd gone with a breathless, "and he's throwing his weight around the *Costa Tarde* board room. They have a Jesús ban now."

I decided to have an early night. As I lay half alive, half dead, trying to sleep, my mind was filled with the image of Don Alvarez José Macasoli and captains of industry like him. He created nothing but wealth and hate. His frightening lack of imagination, a fatal defect in someone in charge of mass communication of any kind, was the direct consequence off hate. Subtly, silently and in secret, hate was gnawing away at him, a bit here today, a bit there tomorrow. There was no contest with love. There can be no contest, for neither passion can co-exist. Once hate takes over control, all is lost. Not many people know that. J.C. does: and knowing he does, I fell into a restful slumber.

I was woken some time in the early morning by a tapping on the apartment door. I'm always wary of unexpected night callers, and when I asked who was there, an indistinct murmur was followed by a louder and more distinct, "It's about Jesús."

I opened the door immediately. The good looking stranger gave me a friendly smile, so friendly I thought for a moment I was being hustled by an escort service, mobile masseur, singing telegram, talking toy boy, dancing rough trade, or any of the other gimmicks by which sex is purveyed like hot potatoes.

"Come in," I said. "But if you're up to no good, I won't hesitate to call the cops."

"Don't you remember me? Diego. The bull fight, the one . . ."

"We took you for dead."

"Jesús refused to let me go."

"What can you tell me about J.C.? Where is he? Is he all right?"

Diego grasped my arms to give me physical reassurance. "I have him over at the *plaza de toros*. He's very weak and exhausted. He's afraid you won't have him back."

"Why not?"

"He thinks you don't understand him."

"Do *you* understand him?"

"Almost. It's to do with the electricity we all have in our bodies in one form or another."

"Tell me more later. Right now, let's get him home and into his bed."

Diego walked with me to the bull ring, which is less than the length of a football pitch from my home. J.C. was sitting in the back of a large, if old Chevvy, its bodywork shined to a mirror surface, two silver bull-horn mascots gleaming on the wings. When he saw me, he tried to get out of the car, but Diego held him back and readjusted the blanket over his shoulders, a necessary protection from the chilly night air coming down from the Sierras. We drove him the short distance to the apartment and between us managed to carry him to his room, undressed him, and put him to bed.

"Explanations in the morning," I said, seeing he was trying to talk. "But right now you're going to have a doctor look you over."

It was as we were getting his arms out of his shirt, I did something I've regretted ever since. I looked at his arms for tell-tale signs of drug abuse. As we lifted him onto the bed, he opened his eyes: truly, they were the windows of his soul. His words, softly spoken, conveyed all the pity in the world.

"You, too, Mister Peter," he said.

I'd swear that at that moment my heart stopped beating as in a frantic panic I began a struggle to survive, a struggle to make my wayward heart protect my thoughtless mind. Dear God, must we for ever destroy the things we cherish most?

"Jesús, save me!" I cried.

Instantly, I felt a power pulse through my body like that gut-tugging surge in the hum of a big amplifier when it's first switched-on. All that remained was awareness that I had just hammered in another nail.

"I'll stay with you till it gets light, but I must be in Seville for the midday casting of the bulls," Diego said. "It's my *alternativa* . . . when I become a full matador."

"Congratulations!"

"It's too bad Jesús won't be there with me."

"He'll be there in spirit," I said. "How did you find him?"

"To tell you the truth, he found us!" He gave a nervous little laugh and I realized some moments later that in spite of his instant success in the bull ring, he had been ill at ease as a guest on a *hacienda* on the Huelva side of the Guadalquivir estuary. Money and class were not on his side: his hosts had even insulted him by offering payment for the exhibition fights he'd given in their corral. "I was out riding with the men," he said, "rounding up the bulls going to Barcelona, when we saw this kid on foot. We assumed he was showing off. I've done it myself without thinking of the danger an initiated bull can be to a matador."

"Which is why you're against running them in the streets – like they do in Pamplona."

"Right. Anyhow, Jesús was in such bad shape I didn't recognize him till we got back to the stables. He refused to go to hospital, so I've brought him to you."

"You did the right thing, thank-you, Diego. But didn't he give you any idea *why* he stayed out there alone, for so long, and with virtually no proper equipment?"

"I was telling you about electricity. Didn't the science master at school make your hair stand on end by brushing it vigorously to produce static? If you lightly place the finger-tips of your right hand to the corresponding finger-tips of your left hand – "

"In an attitude of prayer?"

"Exactly. You can actually *feel* the electricity in your body circulating. Mains electricity in your home is no use to you unless it first goes through some piece of equipment that processes it according to your need."

"Like a radiator warming a room, or a refrigerator keeping our food cool?"

"Right. Jesús has the ability to make people's own electricity work for them. He doesn't perform miracles, *they* do."

"Are you serious? It all sounds like science fiction to me." I was going to add that it also sounded like the basis for yet another kinky religious sect, but I stopped myself in time. I had no right to destroy, confuse or confound faith in whatever guise it may be found.

"Jesús is afraid of the power he feels within him. Every time someone touches him – even a finger-tip on the hem of his jeans – he feels power fly from him. I think that's why he went off by himself. To think it out. He calls it contemplating his belly button."

"You were with him in the wilderness?"

"The twelve of us, yes. We helped to feed the crowd that followed."

"Does he say where he gets this power?"

"It's not unique to him. We all have it, only we don't all know it."

"But where do we get it *from*, Diego?"

"Jesús says, from our father. He makes everything sound so simple."

"I can see I've got to have a complicated talk with him when he's sufficiently recovered," I said.

The doctor finally got round to the night call two hours after I'd phoned. He made no attempt to hide his resentment at being called out for a mere *gitano*.

"These people are very hardy," he said. "Feed him *caldo* for a day, or two, and them go on to solids. You can't include him on *your* membership, you know. I'll have to charge you ten thousand pesetas."

"I'll pay by cheque."
"I'd prefer cash."
"And I'd prefer some bedside manners. You'll get your fee when the company says so. I'll be writing them in the morning."
It wasn't my first clash with the medical profession and I doubted it would be the last. Diego looked acutely embarrassed by the confrontation but he made no comments The rest of the night was occupied making *caldo* and *croutons,* and giving J.C. some nourishment every time he opened his eyes. By the time we'd got a bowlful down him, daylight was penetrating the shutters and Diego decided it was time for him to go.
"I owe him my life," he said. "Look well after his."
The next few days (or was it weeks?) passed in a constant confusion of bedpans, strange faces, invalid diets and phone calls from Don Luis and Mari-Carmen. All my concentration was on looking well after J.C. as Diego had instructed, so much so that I was the last to learn about the virgin of Gorro, who was to enter our lives, whether or not we wished it, with such devastating consequences. The first mention of the incident made no impact on me whatever. I was far too concerned by the growing number of visitors who daily sat at the foot of their master's bed, anticipating an endless supply of *boccadillos* and *cerveza* and resisting all hints from me that a get-well-soon card would be better appreciated by the real master of the house, if not by the temporary usurper of that title.
"He's much better today," the mousy girl said as she was leaving. "Isn't it wonderful how he's always thinking of others? If only he'd stayed there, that poor girl from Gorro may never have died."
The girl rang a bell and I was trying to place her face as I asked, "What girl from Gorro?"
"Why, the crucifix murder," she said, "Surely *you* know all about it, working for the radio as you do."
Suddenly, the bell stopped ringing. I was talking to the cow from Almeria, she of the giant size Chanel No.5, the fair Dolores Madelein. I was about to ask her who the hell

was the virgin of Gorro, when the phone went and I had Don Luis on the line again, pestering me for the umpteenth time to advise the authorities that I'd found Jesús and his name could be struck from the missing persons list.

"If you don't do it soon," Don Luis warned, "they could charge you with wasting police time and then a whole can of worms would be opened up. You don't want to risk his being returned to jail, do you?"

I promised him the earth and was trying to prevent the mousy one from leaving, when Dolores le Grande arrived to check that I was properly looking after her son, and to give him a large tin of *tortas imperial* which, she said, being made of almond, egg-white and sugar, would quickly build up his strength (if, I felt like adding, it didn't as quickly break his teeth). The outcome was that the two women became locked in battle, trying to establish which Dolores was to have the control of J.C.'s life, sublimely unaware that J.C., of all the young men I had ever known, was not susceptible to being controlled by anyone.

"How long have you known Jesús?" the le Grande Dolores wanted to know and, turning to J.C., demanded, "Why don't you tell me about your friends? You treat me more like a total stranger than your mother."

The Madelein Dolores, as I half expected, avoided further conflict with so big a woman and tried to curry favour with her instead. "Jesús tells me you sing in the cathedral," she began; but she got no further.

"I sing in bars, brothels and in my bath," le Grande said. "What do you do?"

"She does her best, mother." Jesús was trying his hardest to heal the rift that had opened up between them.

Le Grande walked over to my drinks cabinet, apparently remembering where it was from the night of the *juerga*. "I have to wash bad words from my mouth," she said. "Will I find a bottle of *fino* here, Peter?"

Like everyone else with whom J.C.'s mum came into contact, I instantly went to do her bidding, and by the time I'd opened a fresh bottle and set out the glasses, I noticed with relief that the mousy Dolores had abandoned the field of battle and had left. I remember thinking she was either recovering from some illness, or was ailing for one. She was certainly in no fit condition to take on le Grande.

"I wasn't interrupting your work, was I?" le Grande asked.

"No, mother."

All thoughts of what I should, or should not, know about Gorro had long fled my mind. Everything had returned to normal, or so I thought. J.C. was up and about, spending a fortune (my fortune, I had to remind him) on phone calls to his friends; I was catching up with correspondence I had neglected, as bread-earning chores for good old Rip-Rip-Hurrah! had to be given priority; and Rafael was coming over from the neighbouring apartment a dozen times a day with one flimsy pretext or another, such was his almost dog-like devotion to his friend.

"I wish I'd been with you on the *romeria,* " he told me. "I'm sure I could have made it, but Jesús convinced me it's my duty to stay and look after my mother and my aunt."

"You're not even using a stick," I said, surprised at his agility after so many years confined to a chair.

"I use a stick when I go out," he said. "Please don't tell Jesús. It would make him angry if he knew. It's not easy, getting confidence, is it? You have to have *some* proof. At least, I do."

Everything was so much back to normal that I woke early with an urge for a bacon-and-egg breakfast instead of my usually hurried coffee. J.C. volunteered to go in search of bacon and eggs, a supply of which we did not have. It was a Sunday morning. Nothing is more dead than the historic centre of Málaga on a Sunday morning. If he could find so much as an over-used wish-bone, it would be a miracle.

"Good luck! You'll need it," I said, carefully avoiding the word 'miracle': I was far from certain J.C. would approve of even a light-hearted suggestion he perform one, just for us.

I was still padding around in my pyjamas when the door bell rang. As I answered it, I heard the distant cathedral clock striking six. Only on Sunday could we hear its comfortably solid sound filling the silent streets. I opened the door, half expecting it was J.C. minus his key as well as being minus eggs and minus bacon; but there was no one there. I was about to blame the two girls who lived with their families three doors away, who lost no opportunity trying to attract J.C.'s attention, when I saw the gaudy cardboard box. It was the kind large dolls are packed in, with phrases in several languages such as 'I cry real tears' and 'I say, "Mamma"'. I knew of no little girl in the building who might be receiving such a present, but left as it was, the wrongful owner would soon be in possession before the rightful owner was awake to greet the day. So I brought it in, hopeful that the thick ladies opposite would be able to help me trace the intended recipient later. The doll was wrapped in a shawl of the most delicate lace, the kind I so often see *gitano* women trying to sell to tourists in Calle Larios or in the park; but for some reason the cellophane box-top had been ripped away. I was about to place it next to the hi-fi console, when it spoke. It didn't actually say, "Mamma", it was more of a gurgle, and the bubbles it blew from its mouth were extraordinarily realistic. I tried holding the box upright to see if it would open its eyes. It did. Warm, brown eyes that were smiling, eyes of real flesh and blood, not glass, as a tiny hand reached out to cling to one of my fingers. The living touch jangled every nerve in my body and I nearly dropped the precious object.

"Somebody left a baby on our doorstep while you were out," I told J.C. when he returned triumphant with eggs, bacon *and* mushrooms. "If they're looking for a home for it, they couldn't have chosen a worse place."

"Isn't he wonderful!" J.C. said, dumping his miraculous Sunday morning shopping on the table and lifting the baby from the cardboard box to hold in his arms. "I'm sure you'll get to like him, Mister Peter."

I scowled at the breakfast ingredients. He surely must have magicked them from a pumpkin, or cajoled them from his two female admirers of three doors away. "It's not going to be here long enough for any deep exchange of personalities."

"Is he despised and rejected of men, then?" Jesús began crooning.

I ignored the allusion. "It's against the law to abandon babies."

"But he won't be abandoned if we look after him."

Now I had to resist his cajoling *me*. " It's also against the law to take in babies as though they were kittens. A damn good cat would be more useful anyhow."

"But he's so defenceless. We must look after him," Jesús insisted.

"You can cut the sentiment," I said, angry because I was beginning to panic. "I'm taking it to the maternity hospital just as soon as we've had breakfast. And what makes you so sure it's a he?"

"Of course he's a he," Jesús said. "And he's going to have his breakfast first. See, there's a feeding bottle in the box and some nappies. All we need is some warm milk."

I was rapidly losing interest in a bacon-and-egg breakfast as I sat there watching J.C. change the baby's nappies and prepare its feed with an assurance that was staggering. I looked at it long enough to establish that it was a boy then, nauseate at the gurgling mess, retreated to the bathroom to do my ablutions.

"Is he ready for walkies?" I asked when I was ready to start the day.

"You can't disturb him while he's sleeping," Jesús said.

"He'd disturb *me* while *I'm* sleeping!" I didn't have to see the dismayed expression to know I was in the wrong. "I'm going for a walk then. Alone. To think."

As I was returning from my walk, little better tempered and even less decided on what to do, I met the two thick ladies on the stairs, dressed in their best, on their way to mass in the cathedral.

"We were woken early this morning by one of your *mozo's* friends, trying to deliver a parcel," Rafael's mum said.

I could feel her irritation. She still resented what J.C.'s friendship had done for her son. "I'm very sorry he disturbed you," I said. "I'll make sure it doesn't happen again."

"It wasn't a boy. It was a young woman," she said. "As if your *mozo* doesn't draw enough attention to himself with his fancy tricks."

I mumbled something about the tricks having to stop and hurried into my apartment. I could hear my *mozo* in my bedroom, apparently talking to the little monster.

"Poor Mister Peter doesn't like babies," he was saying. "He thinks writing silly books and talking on the radio more important. But if you're very, very good, maybe he'll like you enough to let you stay."

"It was dumped on us by a woman," I said, coming into the room. All my shirts had been turned out of the chest of drawers to make a cradle. "I'm giving you till this time tomorrow to find the mother and get this . . . thing . . . out of here!"

"I'm sure she's a very beautiful girl to have a baby such as this one," Jesús said. "She must be a Heredias."

"She's a whore!" My frustration finally exploded.

"She's *not* a whore! She's *not*, she's *not*, she's *not*!" The brown skin round his knuckles whitened with anger as he pummelled the pillow and set about making my bed.

I knew J.C. well enough by now to know this was not the time to push him with questions. If he had something to tell me, tell me he would in his own good time. So I retreated to the word processor to work on a rough outline for the coming Christmas on good old Rip; but I found the presence of a baby in the adjoining room far too distracting. Instead of working, I day-dreamed. When Paul had been alive, we often talked about babies. We had loved each other so intensely he often used to say that if we were not gay we would have had so many kids we'd forget all their names. Maybe, homosexuality is nature's way of birth control, preferable to war, plague or the perversion of a woman's natural functions by medication. Paul had been almost physically thrown out of our doctor's surgery when he pointed out that the contraceptive pill was the first time the medical profession had prescribed for a patient a chemical that caused a malfunction in a healthy body. Paul was certain that in years to come, man will revert to the androgens of his ancestors and Eve, the cockless male, seen to be but a passing hiccup in the great order of things. Possibly in our life time medical science would discover male-male fertilisation and render the female womb as obsolete as the brick oven. It didn't happen in Paul's lifetime and I doubt if it will in mine, but happen it will . . . eventually. For twentieth-century female domination is on the wane. Which will still leave us with the enigma of wanting to make a god in our own image. Man has an insatiable urge to leave a part of himself behind when he dies – a book, a painting, a piece of music, a fine building . . . or a baby.

As I walked over to the bathroom to do a pee, I hesitated by the open door. J.C. was sitting on the edge of the tub, quite naked, holding the naked child in his arms. Sunlight was splashing through the frosted glass window causing halation over the youth's tousled hair and firm brown shoulders. I could hear them exchanging little animal noises of delight. I froze, fearful of disturbing them. After a few minutes, J.C. sensed my presence and looked up.

"I have to go to the *farmacia* to buy talc, or he'll get a rash," he said. "We can use the guest towels for nappies."

"We cannot!" But I knew it had already been done.

After he had dressed, he put the cradle, which a couple of hours ago had been my shirt drawer, on a chair near my desk. "If he cries while I'm out, hold him in your arms and put the bottle in his mouth."

"I'll . . . " I was about to say I'd crack the bottle over the little bastard's head, but I knew I didn't mean it. Besides, in all probability the poor little piece of frail humanity *was* a bastard, unwanted and unloved, the scion of thoughtless, selfish promiscuity. "I've never held a baby in my life," I protested.

"Pretend you're his grandad." He gave me a mischievous smile. "Well, *you* could hardly be his father."

"And why not?"

"Si el viejo pudiese . . . "

If the old man was able . . . It went through me like an avenging sword. My ability, or lack of it, in so many ways.

Nothing I had done in life ever seemed to work out well, never satisfied, never reached its full potential. And now, here was this *gitano* boy, so many years my junior, reminding me that I'd left it too late to be anything other than a father-once-removed from all creation.

"Get out of here! Go and get your talc! And you needn't bother to come back!"

As he left, he came over and kissed me. There was no passion in the kiss, no lust, and no mockery either. I felt love, that tender rebirth of everything good that I had not experienced since Paul had been with me.

"I will be with you always, even unto the end of the world," I heard J.C. whisper. Or was it Paul?

When he'd gone, I began wondering who the baby's father might be. Doubtless some physically attractive but thoughtless young stud who'd create nothing more with his sperm and in all probability had not hung around long enough even to see his creation. And then, the creation began to cry. I had never realized till then what an awesome sound a baby's cry can be. I tentatively lifted it from the cradle and tried rocking it in my arms, but the yells only intensified. I tried sticking the teat of the milk bottle in its mouth and for a moment thought I'd choked it, certain that the little face was turning blue. I was panicking at the prospect of being accused of infanticide when the phone rang.

"Pedro! Have you seen the Sunday papers?" Mari-Carmen's voice was tight with emotion.

"I've had my hands too full . . . "

"What's that noise? Can't you turn the radio down? We've got to talk."

"I've had a baby," I said.

"You must stop making the jokes!"

"I'm not making the jokes. I'm dead serious. It was left on my doorstep. Abandoned. I think it's choking to death, or something. J.C.'s out buying talc."

"Try singing to it."

"*You* sing to it. Go on. He's Spanish. He won't understand rock 'a' bye baby eight to the bar."

Which was how I was brought at last to the full realization of how the virgin of Gorro was about to affect all our lives, holding the plastic receiver to the baby's ear with one hand while the other was trying to turn up the press reports Mari-Carmen was so anxious for me to read. And as I read, I felt my stomach tense and turn. The virgin was the daughter of a wealthy Seville land-owner, one of the most respected families in Spain. She had been staying in Gorro with friends but had gone out riding alone early in the morning. The horse returned seven hours later without its rider. Her body was found three days after that, dreadfully mutilated, with every indication of a sexual attack by someone with a deranged mind. A crucifix had been forced into her womb after intercourse had been completed and twisted and turned till the girl had mercifully died from the loss of blood. The savage murder had been committed shortly after the *romeria* to El Rocio. Gorro was in the desolate marsh land of the Guadalquivir estuary. And the report Mari-Carmen wanted me urgently to see was in *Costa Tarde*. The words seared my eyes and numbed my brain. " . . . *The police are looking for a young* gitano *mystic who was said to be meditating in the area at the time. They believe he can help them with their inquiries.*"

NAVIDAD

IN SPITE OF HAVING lived outside the U.K. in the sun for longer than I've lived inside the U.K. in the cold and damp, I still can't get used to Christmas with iced drinks on the terrace watching bronze-breasted boys on the beach, instead of red-breasted robins in the snow. J.C. had to be dragged to El Corte Ingles to buy our Advent calendar. He didn't say as much at the time, but I don't think he approved my choice of illustration – a polar bear family playing in the snow. And now it was time to tear out the first of the little windows and so eventually reveal the full glory of the nativity scene beneath the surface. Calendars are not for the lonely; and an Advent calendar is a fearful, debilitating sight to one as vulnerable as was I. I almost threw the damned thing away and did what Paul would most certainly have done when he was alive – leave everything, and make the sixty-minute ferry crossing to Morocco, there to swap the ginger wine and plum pud for mint tea and cous-cous in that sober, serene, nerve-calming Moslem paradise; but I knew it would solve nothing, and I had to do something to protect J.C., not so much from a hostile world as from the incriminating influence of his own innocence. I had no idea what was happening to him now, where he might be, who he might be with. All I knew was that I was walking a tight-rope so far as the law was concerned, aiding and abetting a person wanted by the Policia Nacional for questioning in a major murder investigation. That dreadful Sunday when J.C. had gone out to buy talc for the baby; when he returned to the apartment we almost came to blows, arguing over what should, or should not, be done. He wanted to do nothing, absolutely nothing. He was resigned to his fate.

"If our father wants me to be a scapegoat for a mentally ill brother, so be it," was all he would say.

Mari-Carmen had much more to say. As I had still not got round to reporting the missing one found, no one would come looking for J.C. at my apartment, she argued.

She seemed obsessed with the idea that I should do an Anne Frank with him. I had bizarre visions of bricking him up in some secret hide behind the kitchen alcove, which was home to the butano gas bottles. But J.C. resolved the problem his own way.

"Thank you for all you've done for me, Mister Peter," he said. "I'm going now. Our father will look after me."

"You're not to go," I insisted. "Stay till we can work something out."

"I am a *gitano*. If I stay, I can only bring you grief: and I want to give you joy,"

"And I'm a queer! We must work this out together."

He shook his head sadly, "You still don't understand. Before the third Christmas Day peal of bells you will have denied you ever knew me at least three times."

"No, no, no, J.C.. Never! How could you think that of me?"

"You will," he said. And a moment later, he was gone.

I sat for hours in the darkening apartment with the crying baby, stunned by events, paralysed into a state of almost total immobility. At some time late in the night, unable to get any reply to her phone calls, Mari-Carmen arrived with Pippa and banged on my door till I let them in. It was Pippa's idea that to avoid compromising questions from the authorities, which would almost certainly happen if I was to take the baby to the maternity hospital, she and Mari-Carmen would look after it, and at the same time try discreetly to find the mother. I remember Mari-Carmen going into the kitchen and fixing me a glass of hot milk laced with brandy; but I remember little else of that night. They must have put me to bed, because when I woke up I was naked, except for my underpants. The phone was ringing. At first, I couldn't see it; then, I couldn't lift it; finally, I managed to get out a hoarse, "*Digame*."

It was Mari-Carmen. "I *have* to bother you, Pedro," she said. "I'm sorry, but Tio Mac's just told me he wants a particularly scur . . . scur . . . nasty – "

"The word you're looking for is scurrilous, I think. Grossly or obscenely abusive . . . according to O.E.D., that is."

"This scurrilous report went out four times yesterday on the Spanish service. It concerns your boy – "

"He's not my boy. He's not anybody's boy. J.C. is old enough to be the keeper of his own soul. It's just that I don't seem to have looked after him as well as I promised the community I would do."

"As far as Tio Mac is concerned, you most certainly haven't. He wants this scur . . . obscene report translated and re-broadcast after every news bulletin on the English language service. It as good as accuses Jesús of killing the Seville girl. You know how she died?"

"Yes. You don't have to repeat the gory details."

"Tio Mac is insisting all the gory details are repeated in the programme. He's determined that Radio Independiente Plus and that dreadful rag, *Costa Tarde* – I told you he's a director, didn't I? – make a major campaign of it."

"Tell him from me that if he does, I'm not doing any more work for his crappy set-up."

"Too late, Pedro. Sorry, but I'm also to tell you that because of your material and moral support for this kil . . . person, you will never work for us again."

"So, you've told me." I felt a rift opening up between us. "Have *you* anything to add to the little man's pathetic attempt at character assassination?"

I wasn't expecting she would have. I thought she'd already rung off. I was about to put the instrument down, when her voice came over in a whisper against the cacophony going on in the studio. "I think it quite wrong to broadcast statements about people that you know are not true. There's going to be a meeting of the *sindicato* to discuss it. I'll let you know what they decide."

"What *we* decide, please, Mari-Carmen. The day my cigarette nearly set light to the news editor's office, I joined the union."

"Very well . . . tomorrow at eight. I'm father of the chapel, I think that's what you call it in England."

"Yes, mummy."

I was beginning to feel my old self again, thanks to

Mari-Carmen's generous nature and natural tact. It occurred to me how tactful Don Luis had been, not mentioning something the whole of Spain was talking about, because his integrity was such that he knew there was no proof associating J.C. with the savage killing of the virgin of Gorro. I decided to ring him and seek his advice on what I should, or should not, do now.

"Nothing. Do absolutely nothing," Don Luis said. "If a policeman comes knocking on your door, invite him in. Be very polite. Answer all his questions truthfully. You've done nothing wrong. Just go about your affairs in the normal way. It'll all blow over in a couple of days. Everyone is too busy buying last minute Christmas presents to worry about *you*."

"But what do I do about J.C.?"

"Nothing. Do absolutely nothing. He walked out on your generosity, didn't he? Jesús Cepillo Heredias is a very foolish young man, if you want my opinion. I fear these *gitanos* are all the same whether, or not, they're a Heredias. No morals. You do them some good: and what do they do in return? Kick you in the teeth!"

I didn't feel like arguing with him. His opinion of J.C. didn't match my own experience, but I knew the old man meant well. I decided I'd feel better about things if I got out of the apartment, went for a brisk walk through the park and dropped into one of my favourite watering places for a pre-lunch drink. I was in the process of putting on my outdoor shoes, when there was a smashing of glass as a stone came hurtling through the window. My heart missed a beat. What the devil was happening now? I didn't have to wait long to find out. Angry male voices echoed up from the street.

"Amante del gitanos! Maricón! Abajo los extranjeros!"

I had no doubt the abuse was being directed at me. I could hear my heart thumping away as I tried to think coherently. Should I phone for the police? Go down into the street and brazen it out? After all, they didn't intend to do me physical harm, did they? As though to answer my question, I heard a couple of stones bounce off the wall, whoever threw them missing the window glass by inches. I decided to stay where I was, frozen, hiding in my own home, and hope that getting no reaction from me they'd stop their stone-throwing and go away.

All was quiet for the next few minutes, but just when I thought it was safe to look out of the window, there was a knock on the door. I was nearly sick with fear. Then I thought of J.C.. He wouldn't cower in a corner like a hunted animal. J.C. was fearless, protected by some thing or some one. The knocking on my door was repeated. Not loud, but urgent, and it was accompanied by a kind of stage whisper that demanded a reply.

"Rafael! What's going on?" I asked, seeing him standing there, supporting himself with his walking stick.

"It's the Falange, the black shirts," he said. "They make more noise than trouble. I came over to make sure you're all right. They must have heard the broadcast and one of them knew where you live."

"There's an English saying about sticks and stones. I must say words are quite hurtful enough . . . chanted like that!"

"Jesús should not have left you," Rafael said. "He should not have left me."

I was perturbed by the unmistakable resentment in Rafael's voice. "He has to do his thing," I said, somewhat lamely.

He hobbled over to the window and looked out, the rubber tip to his walking stick squeaking with every movement on the tiled floor. "They're going now," he said. "It's best to ignore them. They're no longer a political power and what victories they have are no more than little inconveniences to the rest of us."

"They can whip up the prejudices of people without jobs and without hope," I said. "You shouldn't be so tolerant of the bastards, Rafael."

My getting out of the house didn't make me feel any better about things as I'd hoped it might. The cheerful families lining up outside the *ayuntamiento* in order to file slowly past a model crib of the nativity, which was the same every year, depressed me. The only innovation this year was the repainting of the Virgin Mary, which had placed her ethnic origin some three thousand miles further south than it should have been. Rumour had it that the bishop was so furious when he saw what had been done, that he demanded the crib be closed to public gaze till such a time that the Virgin was reborn further north. But it was a free show; and nothing will prevent Málagueños attending a free show, however paltry, certainly not a mere bishop. I was contemplating the curse of poverty when I saw the police squad car parked outside the entrance to my apartment. Two uniformed men were seated in the car and a heavily built man in a well pressed but ill-fitting suit was on the opposite side of the road, leaning on the low wall that overlooks park and harbour, apparently deep in conversation . . . with Rafael. They both saw me coming at the same time. Rafael hobbled off as fast as his legs could carry him towards the harbour. The policeman came confidently towards me, warrant card in hand, the finger obviously having been pointed at me by Rafael.

"I have reason to believe you know the present whereabouts of one Jesús Cepillo Heredias," he said, wasting no time on pleasantries. "I must warn you that withholding, or giving misleading information to the police, may have very serious consequences."

The two uniformed men had got out of the car. They obviously intended to enter my apartment, with or without the authority of the judiciary, so I led the way. It was only when I was showing them the bathroom, and indicating that J.C. was not lurking in the Ali Baba laundry basket, that I noticed the plastic rattle and teething ring that had been delivered with the baby. The police driver had noticed it, too. I could just make out his eyes behind the dark glasses, looking at me, then at the rattle, then at me again. I thought he was going to say something, but he didn't, either from sheer stupidity or a disinclination to be of any help to a man in plain clothes.

"If Cepillo tries to contact you in any way, or you hear anything concerning his present whereabouts, you must contact the *comisaria* immediately," the inspector said. "Do you understand?"

"Yes," I said, relieved to be closing the door on them.

That evening I turned up early for the meeting of the RIP chapel of the *sindicato*. Like all things Spanish – except the *corrida* – it started late: and then promptly adjourned till after dinner – which meant midnight, at least – as the *Costa Tarde* staff were having a meeting first. In spite of my imminent loss of income, I insisted on taking the father of the chapel out for a meal. I chose the restaurant, a homely Chinese slow-food, and Mari-Carmen chose the menu, a complication of some twenty little dishes, more like Spanish *tapas* than the Chinese meals I remembered in London's East End in my youth. But Mari-Carmen was enchanted by the whole thing, which was what mattered. All the same, the decor and the bouncy way the elderly cashier walked from her desk to the kitchen entrance, where she would keep a vigorous eye on the waiters, was all too reminiscent of the provincial English theatre and Widow Twanky to make my choice of eatery an entirely satisfying one.

"Don't look so miserable, Pedro," Mari-Carmen said. "So far, everything's going well. The night staff on the Spanish service have blacked the tape of that scu . . . scu . . . "

"Scur-ril-ous."

"Yes, scur-ril-ous report, and they're refusing to transmit it again. And now we go and pass a resolution supporting our foreign colleagues. Come."

Albeit was two o'clock Christmas Eve morning before the resolution was drafted, revised, voted upon, drafted again and then voted upon twice; but finally it said what had to be said. The media workers were not going to handle any more lies or distortions demanded of them by Tio Mac. I was no longer isolated. He was. J.C. was no longer a victim. He was. A victim of his own hate.

I decided to walk back to the apartment. It was a clear moonlit night and this, combined with the flood-lighting of the historic buildings – the cathedral, *aduana*, Roman theatre, *alcazaba* – took me back two thousand years. On a night such as this, it was so easy to slip into the shoes of the fisherman. And instantly, I was thinking about J.C. again, where he might be now, where he might be tomorrow and tomorrow and tomorrow . . . I was brought back to reality by having to cross the street to avoid a venomous jumble of Electricidad Sevilliana cables, spitting and sparking live power as they were man-handled back into position to flood-light streets packed with the seasonal *hoi polloi*. I realized I was only a street away from the Slipped Disc and decided to drop in for a night-cap. I knew the atmosphere would be absolute hell on earth; but I plunged into the noise, heat and flashing lights, and wove my way through the phalanx of sweating humanity to the bar. I didn't recognize the hunky young barman but he must have recognized me because he instantly set up a *Cuba libre*, more *libre* than *Cuba*. I'd hardly started to sip than Manolo appeared.

We exchanged the usual seasonal compliments, then he said, "You'll never guess who I've had in tonight."

"No. Who?"

"Your Jesús."

"Christ!"

"Jesús Cepillo, I think, isn't it?" Manolo lowered his voice and brought his lips nearer my ear. "As he's wanted for police questioning, I didn't know what to do. I didn't want to refuse admission as he's your friend. Isn't he?"

"Yes," I said, but I knew my voice lacked conviction. "What did you do?"

"He wanted my upper room. For a private party. There were twelve of them, I think. No, thirteen, according to Ricardo who served them. I told him to make sure it didn't degenerate into an orgy. I have enough trouble with the authorities, as you know, without being had up for keeping a disorderly house. As it was, they only ordered red wine and bread rolls."

"Bread and wine . . . oh, please God, no," I muttered. My attention was caught momentarily by two drag queens camping up some old-time dance.

"Their bill only came to a few thousand, but when Ricardo presented it, Cepillo said to give it to 'our father'. I suppose he meant you." Manolo held out a piece of paper so I could see the total. It was ten thousand five hundred pesetas. Quite enough for bread and wine. I didn't mean to say that, but obviously I must have done, because Manolo ceremoniously tore it up and let the pieces flutter to the floor. "Little Jesús is on the house," he said. "Poor little sod. I wouldn't want to be out there, wandering the streets tonight."

As I came out of the Slipped Disc I saw a group of black shirts pushing towards the entrance. Two of them were carrying a banner that said something about the Virgin of Gorro, 'Avenge Her', or inflammatory words to that effect. Standing just behind me was the uniformed doorman, more of a chucker-in than a chucker-out. I had this very much in mind, when one of the bully-boys spotted me.

"He's the *gitano* murderer's *patron*!"

"*Abajo los extranjeros*!" the cry went up. "*Abajo los gitanos*!"

I joined the chorus. "*Abajo los gitanos*!" I shouted. "Down with them all!"

Their leader, an over-weight slob with a crew cut and drooping moustache, grabbed me by the shoulders. "You know the mother-fucker, don't you?" he roared.

"I know not the man! Now, take your hands off me!"

My Spanish was good enough to make the brute hesitate. I twisted out of his grasp and ran down the street. As I rounded the corner I glanced back. The bully-boys had turned their attention on the Slipped Disc door staff. I was in the clear. I resumed my walk back to the apartment. Away from the night club district sandwiched between the Alemeda and the harbour, the streets were less crowded and I slowed my pace. My feet continued in the direction of my apartment, but my mind was on other things. "I know not the man!" It had come out, just like that. It was the easiest way out of a difficulty, the most comfortable. Why should I have said, "I *do* know him, and I'm proud of it?" More to the point, what should I do *now*? He was being hunted by Tio Mac's rent-a-mob, that was for sure. If they caught him . . . I thought of the many occasions when J.C.'s attitude had always been totally passive, to do nothing, absolutely nothing to protect himself from the greed and malevolence of others. He'd be better off in protective police custody than roaming the dangerous streets. I *had* to help him, I knew that now. I *had* to find him before the black-shirted bully-boys found him.

I was standing in the park looking at the ducks sleeping, each on one leg. It was a little after three . . . in the morning. A night duty plain clothes policeman approached to find out what I was up to at that time of night, recognized me, and stood discussing for some minutes how often a duck changed legs before waking up. He was one of the old-timers who couldn't read too well, and on day duty I'd often seen him sitting in the shade pretending to read the day's newspaper, inadvertently held upside-down. That's it! I bet J.C. has gone up Gibralfaro to a spot Paul always called Upside Down, because to reach it you had to climb a rocky path and then, double back down behind some bushes to reach a kind of open cave with a spectacular view out to sea. And tonight the moon was bright enough to get there without wricking an ankle on the treacherous tracks. It took less than half an hour to get near enough to risk calling his name. I was wondering whether to call J.C., Jesús, or Cepillo, when I saw a flashing blue light coming up the old road, which ends a short distance from the tunnel connecting the *rambla* with Málagueta. Then another blue light, and another, and another. I looked up to the outline of the *parador* sitting beneath the castle wall like a sleeping elephant. The hotel itself was showing no lights but even as I looked, a flashing blue light was reflected on the sombre grey walls. Police were everywhere. A wave of panic swept over me. How was I going to explain my presence, at this unearthly hour, huddled behind a bush halfway up a not-so-mini mountain? No one would believe I was collecting *caracols.* It was too late to move without betraying my hiding place.

The police were using flash-lights now. I caught a glimpse of the leaders climbing up, as a beam from a flash-light belonging to the team scrambling down illuminated them. Guns! The police were armed with automatics! I almost shouted out, you bastards, there's no need for that, you're not hunting a wild animal, merely a boy made in the image of God. And then, I saw another boy. An unmistakable outline even by night, hobbling down the rough track with the aid of his stick, one arm supported by a heavily built policeman. It was Rafael. I had to see what happened, regardless of whether, or not, my presence was discovered. I eased myself from behind the bush, crawling like a rheumaticky tom-moggy towards the rocky edge. There were some tufts of long grass that would provide a modicum of cover. Straining forwards, I could look down into Upside Down hollow: and there they were, J.C. and his little group of . . . delinquents? hobbledehoys? drop-outs? troublemakers? terrorists? As I tried to make up my mind what to think in this vast theatre of nature, where moonlight poured over the heads of her celebrants like sunlight in a cavernous cathedral, I saw the hobbling Rafael, with armed police on either side of him, go close to J.C. and, fumbling, try to hug him. I saw J.C. respond in the full innocence of love. So much evil, sealed for eternity with a kiss, for what reward? The action that followed was swift and painless. The police moved in and arrested J.C.. The other youngsters fled in all directions, the police not attempting to give chase, for they had their man. Only one solitary figure remained. Rafael. He stood silhouetted against the moonlit sea, his whole body visibly shaking, going out of control, till something fled from him and he collapsed like a pile of old rags on the rocky ground.

"Help! Somebody, please help me! I can't walk!!"

I'd come up Gibralfaro to help J.C. and in the event I had to help Rafael. When he saw me his whole nervous system appeared to pack up. His body seemed to weigh a ton. It was quite impossible for me to move him: and all the time he was wailing in a voice that sounded more like a wounded animal than a human being. "What have I done? What have I done . . . done? . . . done?"

"Do you need help there, sir?" It was one of the policemen.

"Am I pleased to see you," I said.

"You two know each other, I take it."

"We're neighbours."

"It's not every day we have the assistance of a foreign resident in catching a villain." He was one of those garrulous cops, liable to talk us both into an embarrassment, so I confined my replies to a simple 'yes', or 'no'. Fortunately, the man flashed for a colleague and the three of us were able to get the wretched Rafael down to the waiting van.

"He's in no condition to give a positive identification, of anything," one of the men grumbled. "What the hell's happened to him?"

The policeman who'd done most of the humping turned to me. "You're neighbours, so you were telling me. Perhaps you could identify the prisoner for us, sir?"

"I know not the man!" I said. "As you said yourself, I'm an *extranjero*. I'm unable to help you. I . . . I . . . want to be alone!"

Monstrous as my performance was, the Garbo bit actually worked. The senior of the men saluted me and as I walked with gathering speed towards the tunnel and the city centre, I told myself I'd have been no help to J.C. if I had given them a positive identification. Nevertheless, the words I couldn't get out of my mind were his words. "Before the third Christmas Day peal of bells . . . " Reject, reject, reject! Why did I have this compulsion to destroy the very thing I wanted to possess? And for the first time in my life the answer was crystal clear. Fear. I was terrified of the purging power of love.

I must have wandered about the city aimlessly for four or five hours, because the next thing I can recall was my return to the empty apartment. I was turning the key in the lock when Rafael's mother appeared in her doorway.

"We were so worried about you," she said. "We were afraid you'd been arrested and it would have been so unfair if you had been. After all, you did more than was expected of you for your *mozo* . The *gitanos* are all the same. If they thought they could get away with it, they'd murder you in your bed."

I didn't argue with her. I didn't feel like arguing with anyone. "How's Rafael?" I asked. "I'm afraid last night was a great strain on him."

"I gave him one of his sedatives," she said. "He's sleeping now. My sister helped me get his wheel-chair out. It's fortunate we didn't sell it."

"Very fortunate," I murmured. She was blissfully unaware of the true nature of the drama. All that concerned her was that things had returned to normal. They'd had their cross returned to them.

As soon as I entered the apartment, J.C. filled my mind. His presence was everywhere, little things that he liked (such as the china screwing-donkeys Paul and I had brought back from a holiday on Capri, or the cushion he always seized when we settled down for an evening's TV) I couldn't get away from them. Finally, they drove me out into the streets again. I felt like drinking myself into oblivion but I knew this would not help J.C., so I settled for black coffee, not one, not two, but a coffee in every cafeteria I could find open, for many in the city centre never opened Sundays and festivals. A rapid build up of caffeine on top of the nervous exposure of the past few days was certainly not what any doctor would order. I was like an over-wound alarm-clock, my spring so tightly confined I was liable to break out at any moment.

'Armed police have arrested a man they want to question about the virgin of Gorro murder . . . '

I heard the news on the radio while I was nervously stirring sugar into my fifth, or possibly sixth coffee. How were they questioning J.C.? I'd heard so much about Spanish police brutality, mostly referring to the bad old days of the Franco dictatorship, or to the more recent terrorist activities of the Basques in that cold and wet corner of Spain up north. Surely they wouldn't ill-treat J.C.? They wanted to pin a murder on him, wasn't that ill-treatment enough? I knew I had to do something to help him, but what? I decided to phone Don Luis.

"There's nothing we can do more than I've already

done," he said.

"*You've* done! What have you done?"

"I've just come from the *comisaria*. I tried to get you at home but there was no reply."

"You've seen J.C.? I presumed you were no longer interested in representing him. After all the trouble he's caused you."

"Because I don't like his attitude doesn't mean I am prepared to abandon my professional responsibilities towards him." Don Luis sounded very tired, or suddenly very old. "But I fear he doesn't want my representation. He doesn't want any representation. He keeps on about our father being the only representative he needs. What does he mean by that? Do you know what he means by that?"

"He can be very . . . deep, Don Luis," I said. "They're not going to be rough with him, are they?"

"Not unless he's rough with them. No, he won't come to any physical harm in the *comisaria*, but I fear he may let them talk him into an admission of something he most certainly did not do."

"Do you think they will let me see him?"

"I very much doubt it. They only let me have five minutes with him because the law says every citizen has a right to legal representation."

My mind was made up. "I'll go down there now and try," I said. "I feel so inadequate, doing nothing."

As I came out of the cafeteria I found myself in the centre of another lot of Tio Mac's fascist bully-boys. They weren't interested in me. Their attention was focused on a *gitano* woman and a couple of young girls who may or may not have been her daughters. The women had a basket of fine lace work they had been trying to sell to tourists. The tourists had fled and the bully-boys were laughing and using foul language as they tore and ripped the delicate needlework. One of them, displaying no trace of shame, took out his penis and urinated over the remaining items in the women's collection of needlework. Then, laughing among themselves, the bully-boys went on their way. The woman squatted on the pavement and began sorting out her ruined lace, while the eldest of the two girls started to sing a popular Andalusian Christmas carol.

> * *Campana sobre campana,*
> *y sobre campana una;*
> *asomate a esa ventana,*
> *veras a un niño en la cuna.*
> *Bélen*
> *Campanas de Bélen*
> *que los angeles tocan.*

Her voice had the strength and purity that is common to the southern Spaniard; but now she had real cause to sing with controlled passion of the pain and poverty and need that lies just beneath the surface of a seasonal carol. Very soon she had gathered a large audience and a swarthy man in red striped trousers and a gold ear-ring, began collecting donations. They had snatched a little victory out of a major defeat. Indeed life is a constant downhill struggle. I tried to shake the word '*campana*' from my mind. The accusation that I was insincere, shallow, a turn-coat, in short, a bastard, was not the way I wanted the world to see me: but it was the way J.C. saw me and had warned me . . . the three peals of bells on Christmas Day.

"I need you, Jesús. If, when I get to the comisaria *I find you don't exist, that you're only a ghost, that nothing happened in the magical moonlight up Gibralfaro last night, I shall still need that ghost, that spirit to cling to, in order to look into the mirror of life and see where I have gone so dreadfully wrong."*

"I'm sorry, sir, but it is not possible for you to see

> * The bells ring out,
> The bells ring out;
> Look through that window,
> You will see a baby in the cradle.
> Bethlehem
> The angels are ringing
> The bells of Bethlehem.
>
> -Trad.

Cepillo, even if the courts did make an order putting him in your charge." The inspector was choosing his words carefully. "We hope to be making a statement to the media tomorrow. I see no reason why you shouldn't be present for that. You *are* a radio personality, are you not, sir?"

No, sir was not a radio personality any more, but I didn't tell the man that: it was obviously no use pushing him any further, so I wandered round the *comisaria* till I found the public waiting room and bar. I just sat, picked up a day-old newspaper and stared at it, trying to force myself into thinking what I was going to do. Just sitting and worrying was not going to get me anywhere: and it would certainly not help J.C..

"Buenos dias, señor."

I looked up to see a young face I knew I should recognize, but it didn't click.

"Fernando. *Costa Tarde*."

"Piss off! Don't you think you've caused me enough trouble already?"

But he didn't piss off. "I'm not responsible for what our owners do," he said. "I guess you haven't seen him, or you wouldn't be sitting here."

"Correct. You have seen him, I suppose?"

"Yes. My sister's the duty *abogada* and she was able to fix it for me."

A female lawyer. That would put old Don Luis's nose out of joint, if he knew. "How is he? They're not beating him, or anything like that, are they?"

"He's fine. He gave me an exclusive," the cub reporter said enthusiastically. "But I doubt if that bastard Tio Mac will let us run it. The editor's on the verge of handing in his resignation as it is."

"Tell me about J.C.," I insisted.

"He's in the clear. They'd like to pin a murder on a *gitano* but they know they can't."

"Why? Do they know who *did* kill the girl?"

"They know he couldn't have done. They had blood and sperm samples taken from the scene of the crime. It wasn't the victim's blood and neither was it the blood of Jesús. It was group A. Very common. Jesús it seems is group B. Very rare. And the sperm was not Jesús's sperm either."

"So what happens next?"

"The Civil Governor has seen him and is refusing to have him sent to Seville. He said he could find no fault in the man. He's washed his hands of him. There's nothing else they can get him on, so they'll have to let him go."

"When?"

"Just as soon as Seville accepts the situation. Which could be any time. No one's very pleased about it. They *want* to blame the *gitanos*. They'll blame the *gitanos* for anything if they can. They're already blaming them for the lack of rain."

I walked with the youngster down the labyrinth of *comisaria* corridors till eventually we found ourselves outside in the winter sunshine. On the opposite side of the street was a crowd being prevented from crossing to the *comisaria* side by police barriers and half a dozen Policia Nacional in riot gear. Four of the demonstrators were carrying a large banner made from what looked like an old bed sheet. On it was a crude drawing of a figure supposed to be J.C.. He was wearing a surplice and had a halo over his head; but in his right hand was a dagger and in his left a crucifix, both dripping red-paint blood. The slogans on either side of the drawing were being chanted by the crowd. *ABAJO LOS GITANOS! VENGA LA VIRGEN DEL GORRO. PENA DE MUERTE.* Chanting, clapping their hands and stamping their feet in a primitive tribal rhythm. Vengeance. Violence. Retribution. Legalized murder. They wanted it all. They had to have someone to blame for their sins and they wanted those sins destroyed. Totally. Kill, kill, kill . . .

The young reporter must have seen the fear in my face. "Don't worry, *señor*. The police will control them. They will get tired soon and go home to make ready for the festival."

"When do you think he'll be released?"

"Most likely when they have a conference for the media in the morning, at ten. They'll make a big thing about forgiveness at the season of goodwill. It'll make the local police look good."

If the reporter's information was correct, and I had no reason to believe otherwise, by this time tomorrow J.C. would be back with me and we could celebrate Christmas together, as Paul and I had always celebrated Christmas. Together. It was still not too late to do some Christmas shopping. I walked to my favourite supermarket and spent a joyous half-hour piling a trolley with all the exotic extravagance of the season. I found I'd bought so much, I had to have a taxi back to the apartment. I felt so elated, I settled down and started to put on some LPs of music I always used to enjoy this time of the year – Berlioz's *L'Enfance du Christ*, Britten's *A Child Was Born* and the like. I finally exhausted myself and fell into bed about midnight. The phone woke me and even before I answered it I knew something bad had happened.

"This is Fernando, *señor*."

"Who?" I was struggling to clear my mind.

"Your reporter friend. It's about Jesús. He's been released. They let him out at one this morning."

"Where is he now?"

"I don't know. No one seems to know. All the media are trying to find him. I hoped you might know."

"Is anyone else trying to find him? That's what worries me."

There was a moment's silence. "Tio Mac's still putting out the poison. Radio Independiente Plus last night was demanding the Civil Governor's resignation. And our paper this morning is running a banner headline GOVERNOR PLAYS PILATE."

"If you find him before I do, tell him to go at once to the nearest *comisaria* and telephone me from there. He's to take the duty sergeant's number and not to let them leave him alone till I collect him."

I was girding my loins for battle, determined to be the Knight in Shining Armour who would take unto himself the thrust of Arthur's Excalibur, the parry of Parsifal's spear, and so do battle against the Prince of Darkness. I told myself I'd been taking life much too seriously of late.

No one meant J.C., or me, any real harm. No one took J.C.'s larking about all that seriously. No one thought him capable of murder. Did they? As I got my legs across my favourite Harley steed and felt him roar to life, it all came together like old times, when Paul had been with me. Then we used to get up early Christmas morning to ride up the tracks behind the city to watch the miraculous birth of the sun from atop the *montes*. Miracle . . . or optical illusion? Concentrate! Clear your mind! Thinking logically about J.C., I began circling the city systematically in an urgent attempt to find him. Wouldn't it be better to stay peacefully at home, and not roam about the world seeking better bread than is made of wheat, never considering that many go for wool and come back shorn? The Knight of the Sad Countenance was riding pillion and whispering in my ear. Take care, your worship, those things over there are not giants but windmills. Then, as I turned left by the flood-lit parish church of San Miguel de Miramar, I saw the first glimmer of dawn illuminating the faithful going to mass. And I heard the first peal of Christmas bells.

"Pe-dr-oo!"

I only just heard the shouting out of my Spanish name. I jammed on the brakes and looked about me. A solid purple mass was waddling towards me. It could only be Mari-Carmen. The studios were just a stone's throw away; but I'd never thought of her as the mass-going type. And royal purple was a bit much, even for Christmas.

"Pedro, thank goodness I've seen you. I left a message on your answering machine. You've heard about Jesús?"

"Yes, he's been released,"

"And have you heard on the news, what they're calling a citizen's committee . . . they're in the city centre, forcing any *gitano* they see to leave the area."

"Leave where to? Where do they expect them to go?"

"The shacks near the municipal tip, apparently. That's where they've always had to go."

"That's Tio Mac's idea, is it?"

She gave me a helpless little shrug. "The *sindicato* has done its best. I'm sorry, Pedro, I can't do more."

"If J.C. has a mark on him, if it's the last thing I do, I'll see he rots in an early grave!" I pushed the Harley off its stand and gave it a kick. "Say an Ave Maria for me, or whatever it is you do, and thanks from us both for your help."

I was riding slowly up and down the depressing shanty town, a place tourists were never shown and residents never wanted to see, when I heard a second peal of Christmas bells. Harsh, tuneless iron bells that suited the neighbourhood well. A couple of refuse trucks were grinding their way noisily up a hill made by years of tipping. The wood, cardboard, and tin shacks were bulging with raggedly-dressed, dark-skinned people who overflowed into what had to pass for a street. A Bedford van with no wheels and an abundance of rust had been turned into a general store: there was no sign of any other shop. In the opposite direction to the man-made hill was a piece of flat no-man's-land, unwanted and unloved, on which were several modern villas, dilapidated and boarded up, with *prohibida la entrada* signs every few yards. A dusty, faded announcement indicated they were an urbanization intended for retired Scandinavians which went bust before it blossomed. A few children began to approach my pride-and-joy, but were dragged back into the shade of the shacks by suspicious, or hostile, adults. I had no doubt this was a no-go area for the *policia,* or if not no-go, seldom-come. I was beginning to think I was wasting time looking for J.C. here, when a refuse truck coming down the hill gave me a couple of blasts on his horn.

"Are you looking for the skinny miracle-maker, *hombre*?" the driver shouted, pushing a dust-covered head out of his cab. "If you are, you'd better hurry!"

The Harley roared angrily up the steep incline. At the top, the ground shimmered with silver from the thousands of crushed cans daily polished by truck tyres. The sun, already bathing the silver with shafts of gold, went behind a cloud. The man-made heaven came to an abrupt end with a cliff-like fall, down which the trucks tipped their waste. At the furthest corner, on the very edge of the precipice, I saw twenty, or thirty, people gathered round a slender youth. Several cars were parked a short distance from them. As I came closer, I could see it definitely was J.C.: and the men were similar to, if not the same bully-boys of Tio Mac's rent-a-mob. J.C. was in a pathetic state. His hands were tied behind his back. His green shirt was ripped in several places and spluttered with blood. On his head, at a crazy angle, was a cracked and upturned po. I leant the Harley on its stand. As I approached, a distant peal of church bells seemed to freeze both victim and adversaries. It was the third peal I'd heard that morning . . . and I'd not denied him. I could never deny him again. At that moment, J.C. saw me standing there. His eyes were full of gentle acceptance . . . of everything.

"Stop whatever you're doing at once!" I yelled.

A heavy brute in black leather and chain jewellery snarled, "He says his father will look after him, so he's going over the top and daddy can have him!"

Another, brandishing a thick piece of splintered wood, hissed, "Tell us how you do the water into wine trick. Go on, tell us, or do you want some more stick?"

And a third, "You're a stinking *gitano* pervert! Now, let us hear you say it, what are you?"

This was the moment when I should have leapt into action, taken them all on with bare fists, and have the situation well under control by the time the cops, fire brigade and paramedics arrived. But life is not like that. I was out of shape, no fit match for even one of these slobs; and I had no reason to suppose the friendly truck driver would have called the police, or if he had done, I had no reason to suppose they would hurry to a no-go area.

What happened next was an accident for which I could never blame the mob, blame J.C., or blame myself. I reached out to take J.C.'s hand and lead him away with the intention of daring anyone to stop me. The bully with the chain jewellery made to grab my arm but slipped on the highly polished metal, knocking J.C. off balance and sending him backwards over the edge of the tip.

"May God forgive you, forgive all of you," I said,

leaping on the Harley.

"You'll see him flying up with his fairy wings if he can work miracles," the one with the splintered wood said.

I raced down the dirt track at the side of the tip, but was stymied when it suddenly disappeared under the piles of rubbish. I expected to see J.C. laying on top of it; but he wasn't. I looked up and saw him dangling from a tangle of power cables. The cables had been looped on temporary posts from the substation behind me by Electricidad Sevilliana, taking the shortest route to flood-light the city centre. J.C. was wriggling in an effort to free his hands from their bondage, untangle himself from the cables, and fall and slide and slither down the lower half of the tip to safety. I saw the wrists part, but just at that moment what at first looked like a coil of rope came hurtling from above.

"Here's your crown of thorns, Jesús!" a voice echoed from somewhere out of sight. "Take care how you put it on!"

A burst of laughter was drowned by J.C.'s sudden cry of anguish, as the length of barbed wire twisted itself over his trapped body, simultaneously making contact with the exposed copper wire of one of the power cables where it was inadequately lashed to the temporary post. There was an instant flash, and J.C.'s body seemed to dance in space before at last coming to rest, arms outspread, hanging from the twisted cables. There was a constant sparking from the ancient insulators on the post. J.C.'s body twitched once or twice more, and then was still. Very still. The clouds overhead darkened so that it was almost night and a few heavy drops of rain heralded the storm to come. I heard voices behind me as a crowd gathered, curious to find out what was happening. In the distance, a police siren reminded me of the living world, for at this moment I was no longer in it. I was with J.C. in death. A blinding flash of lightening came down from above, followed by a roar of thunder that I discovered later had shaken every building in the city. Man and nature were one, as I heard a voice within me cry, "Fear not, for I will be with you always, even unto the end of world."

LOS REYES

JESÚS CEPILLO HEREDIAS was buried the following day at a simple ceremony in Alora. His mother and father treated me as another son and, shocked though I was, I felt like J.C.'s brother, for his last gift to me had been understanding. I saw life as he, in the full flood of youth, saw life: an inextinguishable flame. By which he understood the disease of the diseased, the darkness of the blind, the silence of the deaf, the misery of those who live only for pleasure, and the total poverty of the wealthy. My Jesús loved life and feared not death. The world was too small for his capacity to love: there was no room for hate to take root within him. He performed no miracles; for what he did was as logical as the coming of spring, and even more beautiful. His mere presence brought peace to those in anguish, so that to touch a hem of his clothing, or to feel his hand glance their skin, was enough for them to forget all pain. When he opened the eyes of the blind, it was to show them life: and those who heard nothing but the noise of drugged excess, heard the sounds that satisfy. When he spoke, people forgot their hunger: and plain water had the taste of good wine. Frustrating passions fled at his approach: and those whose lives were dead from boredom and lost imagination, if imagination there had ever been, rose from their grave-like lethargy when they saw him. So it was not the least surprising that after we had buried J.C. his friends and relations crowded into the small house in Alora where José, the father, got out his guitar, and Dolores, the mother, burst into song. The party glowed with good wine and companionship till, by nightfall, so many people had arrived to become a part of it, the celebration moved into the next door house and so on down the street, till the whole of Alora seemed to be honouring the memory of the *gitano* Jesús.

There were still four more days to go of the twelve days of Christmas. The children had not received their presents yet for by tradition they received their gifts on the morning of January 6th, to some people, Epiphany, but to the Spanish, Los Reyes. Every town and village has its carnival procession at which the Kings shower the children with candies from their colourful floats. The Spanish make sure the twelve days are also twelve nights, coming to a climax New Year's Eve with the *Extraordinario Cotillon de Nochevieja* with its *uvas de la suerte*, lucky grapes, on which Paul once nearly choked to death, trying to get all twelve down him as the cathedral clock struck the midnight hour. It is not a time to be alone. After the excesses of J.C.'s Spanish wake, I braced myself for a dark void of unemployed loneliness. But it didn't happen. Dolores le Grande phoned me from Alora every day, making it clear that I would always be more of a son than just a friend to her. The two thick ladies opposite baked fresh cakes every day and either Rafael's mum, or his aunt, would sit with me while I consumed gargantuan portions, which they said I had to do to build up my strength. Manolo sent several bottles of my favourite tipple on several different occasions by several different young couriers, till I wasn't sure if the intended gift was bottle, or boy.

Then Mari-Carmen made a state visit, accompanied by Pippa. That, I thought, was going to be acutely embarrassing, but she broke the ice by dropping a teapot I've always hated on the tiled floor. I'm pleased to say it was beyond repair and after we'd mopped up the mess we settled for instant coffee.

"Pedro, as father of the chapel I've had words with Tio Mac."

"Oh, yes . . . " I was far from delighted with the prospect of eating humble pie. The man's money and his prejudice had contributed to J.C.'s death, even if it hadn't been the direct cause.

"He didn't expect anyone to get killed. He didn't *want* anyone to get killed. He admits he was wrong, jumping to conclusions over the death of the Seville girl as he did."

"Go on . . . "

"And – well, in short, Pedro, he has withdrawn his demand for your resignation and has agreed we should do

a regular programme about the *gitanos*."
"Gay *gitanos*?"
"All *gitanos*."
"I'll think about it," I said. "By the way, what's happened to the baby? Have you found the mother yet?"
"We think we've found two fathers." She must have seen my raised eyebrows because she added, "You'll be the first to know, I promise."
I was. It was the morning of Los Reyes when everyone breakfasts on a spicy cake made in the shape of a crown and decorated with crystallised fruit jewels. I was woken at eight by a knocking on the door. When I answered it, I found a mousy young woman standing there with what looked like a brand new Rolls Royce of a perambulator.
"Good morning, Mister Peter. King cake?"
She pushed the perambulator into the apartment before I could refuse admission and took out a large, expensive looking King cake. But I wasn't looking at the cake. My eyes were fixed very firmly on the baby sleeping underneath it.
"That's baby Jesús," she said. "His daddy would like him to be taught English by you, as his daddy was taught English . . . by you."
"You're Dolores Madelein . . . of course . . . and this little monster I've seen before . . . it's J.C.'s son."
As I picked the baby up and held it nervously in my arms I heard the mother say, "Can we stay? Please, to look after you. J.C. promised he'd be with you always."
I could hear J.C. whispering within my very being . . . "even unto the end of the world." How could I say no to love?

. . . the end of the beginning

THE WIDOWED TIA TULA, who helps her married sister run the *posada* in Pavo has ended the day by insisting that her brother-in-law is a *lobo* because he goes out alone at night to prowl with other *lobos*. She warns her sister that when he returns the door is not to be opened on the first knock, it is dangerous as he might attack them. When he knocks for a second time, she must still not open the door, or she will see him with a man's body and a *lobo's* head. Only on the third knock is it safe to let him in.

The old men sit in the shade of the oleanders in the Plaza de la Constitution (formerly José Antonio, formerly just the *plaza*) and nod their heads. This they know to be true because their forefathers told them so.

The day Franco died, Jesús was born. In Pavo.

GLOSSARY

The following Spanish words used in the story may not all be familiar to the reader:

Abajo	down with
Abogado	lawyer
Aduana	Customs House
Aficionados	enthusiasts
Albariza	type of soil
Alcazaba	fortress
Amante	lover (of)
Alternativa	when *'novillero'* becomes *'matador'*
Amor Brujo (El)	'love-potion'
Andalusia/Andaluz	8 southern provinces of Spain
Armada	navy
Autopista	motorway
Aviso	notice
Ayuntamiento	Town Hall
Banderillas	darts used in bullfight
Banderilleros	men who place darts
Bastón	ceremonial stick of gypsy elder
Besugo	sea bream
Boccadillo	sandwich
Bodega	wine cellar
Bonita!	pretty one!
Bota	wine-skin
Brik	' box' of wine, milk etc.
Buenos dias	good morning
Buleria	a flamenco song style
Butano	bottle gas
Burro	donkey
Cabo	police sergeant
Cal	lime wash
Càldo	broth
Calamares	fried squid
Calle	street
Campana	bell

Campo	countryside
Carabineros	armed with rifles
Caracol	snail (3-wheel vehicle)
Cárcel	jail
Casa	house
Casa mata	cottage
Caseta	booth / stall at fair
Caudillo	leader
Cava	EU designated name for Spanish 'champagne'
Cerveza	beer
Chanquetes	small fried fish
Chica(o)	girl / boy
Chiringuito	beach bar
Chorizo	paprika sausage
Churros	fried doughnuts
Ciega(o)	blind person
Cinco	five
Cofradias	associations
Comedor	dining room
Comisaria	police station
Copa	glass / a drink
Copla	flamenco verse
Corrida	bullfight
Costa del Sol	Sunshine Coast
Coto	protected land
Cuadrilla	bullfighter's team
Cuba libre	rum and cola
Cucaracha	cockroach
Desayuno	breakfast
Digame	'phone 'Hello!'
Dos amigos	pair of motorcycle police
Duende	goblin, elf
Duro	ancient 5pts coin still used (illegally) in pricing
Español	Spanish
Espato	coarse grass
Extranjeros	foreigners
Farmacia	pharmacist

Feria	fair
Fino	fortified wine of Jerez
Flamenco	gypsy song, dance and life-style
Franco	Gen. Francisco Franco, Spanish dictator 1939-1975
(con) Gas	bubbly mineral water
(sin) Gas	still mineral water
Gato	cat
Gitano	gypsy
Gordo	fat
Gripe	influenza
Grua	(tow-away) crane
Guapo!	good-looking, super
Guardia	(Civil) green uniformed foreign incident police
Hasta luego	see you later
Hermandad(es)	brotherhood(s)
Hola!	hi!
Holgazanear	idling
Huevos	eggs
Jamón (serrano)	ham (cured)
Jefe	boss, chief
Jerez	fortified wine of the region (sherry)
Jondo	deep, profound (of song)
Juerga	rave-up, gig
Jumilla	wine from Murcia district
Juntadora	tester, examiner
Lucio	pike
Lobo	wolf
Magdalenas	buns
Maletilla	'little suitcase'
Manzanilla	a kind of 'sherry'
Maricón	vulg. queer
Matadero	abattoir
Merienda	afternoon tea
Merodear	prowling
Montes	hills
Mozo	young man, porter

Muleta bullfighter's red 'rag'

Navidad Christmas

Nazareno Easter penitent

Novillero apprentice bullfighter

Nuevo new

Olé! Bravo!

ONCE Spanish organisation for the blind

Padrinos best man,godparents

Panaderia bakery

Pañuelo handkerchief

Parador state owned hotel

Paseo Sunday walk or avenue

Pase natural bullfighter's movement

Pasodoble tempo of bullfight music

Payo gypsy name for non-gypsy

Pena penalty

Permiso permit

Picador mounted bullfighter with lance

Pipa del campo country pipe

Piropos poetical 'bottom-pinching'

Pitos flamenco finger-snapping

Policia National police and Municipal police

Pollo vulg. penis

Por favor May I?

Portes goods taxi

Posada country inn

Prohibida la entrada no entry

Pruebe proof

Pueblo village

Puerta doorway

Rambla dried-up river

Rastro flea-market

Reyes kings

RENFE Spanish railways Red Nacional de Ferrocarrilas Espana

Rocieros those on pilgrimage to E1 Rocio

Romeria pilgrimage

Saetas flamenco religious song

Salas de fiesta	night club / disco
Salchichon	salami sausage
Sangria	fruit drink with alcohol
Seco montes	dry 'mountain' wine
Semana Santa	Holy Week (Easter)
Señor(a)(ina)	Mr, Mrs and Miss
Sevillana	type of flamenco dance
Simpecado	copy of religious emblem
Sindicato	trade union
Sol/Sombre	sun / shade
Supermercado	supermarket
Sur	south / Diario Sur, the Málaga newspaper
Tamborileros	travelling musicians
Tapas	tit-bits with drinks
Tarde	after lunch but before dinner
Tia(o)	aunt / uncle
Tonto	idiot / fool
Toros	bulls
Torre	tower
Tortas imperial	a kind of nougat
Trono	throne
Ultimas	latest
Uvas	grapes
Vagabundo	vagrant
Venta	country restaurant
Veronica	bullfighter's movement
Vivienda	place to live
Zapateado	flamenco foot-stamping
Zarzuela	operetta

Also available

The Cruelty of Silence

Sebastian Beaumont

The Cruelty of Silence is the highly anticipated new novel from the author of *On the Edge, Heroes Are Hard to Find* and *Two.* This subtle and intensely atmospheric novel begins on the anniversary of the enigmatic disappearance of successful architect Alex Stern. His lover, Lol, has to spend a deeply distracted year looking for him – at the cost of both his job and of the comfortable home they shared. After much frustration and an inability to restart his life, Lol discovers that a large sum of money is missing and that a locked computer file may contain the vital clue to what really happened to Alex. Set in Edinburgh, Spain, Paris and Amsterdam, *The Cruelty of Silence* is a taut and compelling contemporary mystery. It is also a striking account of the rewards and tensions of family life, the confusion created by new love, of pop music and drugs . . .

ISBN 1-873741-30-8

£9.50

Thresholds

David Patrick Beavers

Set in early summer 1977, *Thresholds* is at once a claustrophobic and intensely sensual novel about three eighteen year olds idling away time as they decide what to do with their lives. Brian has been left Kehmeny Court, a house with rambling grounds, on the Pacific coast near San Francisco. Living with him are his fiancée Viola and his best friend Morgan. Everything should be idyllic – but discontent is about to bring change. Brian is falling out of love with Viola and, perhaps, in love with Morgan. Meanwhile Morgan, who has been in love with Brian since childhood, finds love now becomes sexual. David Patrick Beavers – author of *Jackal in the Dark* and *The Jackal Awakens* – focuses on the erotic turmoil that seems so much a part of late adolescence to produce a novel that is nostalgic, powerful and stimulating.

ISBN 1-873741-28-6

£8.50

Oddfellows

Jack Dickson

Oddfellows marks an auspicious debut for Scottish novelist Jack Dickson. This is the story of Joe Macdonald, dishonourably discharged from the army, who becomes a bouncer for – and lover to – nightclub owner and entrepreneur Billy King. Their relationship is all about power – Billy commands, Joe obeys. But when Joe intervenes after Billy commits a particularly brutal rape of a fourteen year old, things become more uncomfortable. And not just for Joe. Drawn into this web of double dealing, violence and murder are Joe's teenage nephew Sean and appealing policeman Andy Hunter. Located in Glasgow's gay and criminal underworlds and encompassing child abuse, drugs and sado-masochism, *Oddfellows* is a starkly delineated novel about aspects of gay life that many would rather ignore.

ISBN 1-873741-29-4

£9.99

Brutal

Aiden Shaw

Now in its third edition, *Brutal* is a raw and powerful debut novel which explores the life of a young man who makes a living as a prostitute. Paul, with the help of therapy, is trying to challenge what he has become – a person out of control on drugs and alcohol, desiring abusive and degrading sex, estranged from people he once loved. Moreover, he is facing his own mortality while living with H.I.V. Increasingly disappointed by the way men relate to each other, he discovers that there are women around him to whom he cam turn.

Set mainly in London's underground club scene – where drug use is commonplace and casual sex something of an inevitability -*Brutal* offers an extraordinary, sometimes bleak portrait of a lost generation for whom death is as much a companion as lovers, friends, and family. Yet this is far from being a dispirited novel, and although the subject matter may shock, the shining honesty of the writing will prove life-affirming and an inspiration.

ISBN 1-873741-24-3

£8.50